Damian Cloutman has struggled with dyslexia his whole life, but with effort and the right help when he reached secondary school he was able to better himself. He hopes that this book will inspire others with dyslexia to try harder to show everyone that they can be just as intelligent.

Damian Cloutman

SHADOW OF MAGIC

AUSTIN MACAULEY
PUBLISHERS LTD.

A CIP catalogue record for this title is available from the British Library.

ISBN 9781786125217 (Paperback)
ISBN 9781786125224 (Hardback)
ISBN 9781786125231 (E-Book)

www.austinmacauley.com

First Published (2017)
Austin Macauley Publishers Ltd.
25 Canada Square
Canary Wharf
London
E14 5LQ

I would like to thank my late grandfather, William David Strange; his inner strength gave me the idea for the main character. My nephew, Dayton Dennis Stephen William Muir, for being my lucky charm. I would also like to thank my parents, Stephen and Diane Cloutman, as well as my sister, Montanna Cloutman, and my wife Sheemah Cloutman, for their constant support.

Chapter One

Mithos and his class waited outside the classroom for Professor Lucian Rohnal, head of the advanced student department. He had left them waiting for ten minutes before they saw him coming down the hall in his red silk trench coat embroidered with black flames.

'Sorry, hope I didn't keep you waiting too long,' he said. It irritated Mithos how he could always say that with a smile.

Lucian opened the door, inviting the class inside. Mithos always thought it was too big for six students but they were the only ones advanced enough to handle the lessons. Even though the professor was kind in helping where he could and always greeted them with a smile, he was a tough teacher. Some of his lessons taught the pupils spells that were deadly if the slightest error was made when casting.

'OK, class, you have each mastered at least one element of magic so now I will give you all a pop quiz! Amanda, could you tell me why the five schools of Magic were created?' asked the professor. The girl with white hair stood up.

'The five most powerful countries were constantly at war and they all used Mages. So in order to stop the endless battles, the five most powerful wizards brought the five great nations together and it was agreed that there would be five schools created, one for each country. They would be independent and not ruled by any one man but by the magic council. This brought an end to the wars and led to many of the most dangerous spells being named as forbidden.'

He seemed pleased with her answer.

'OK, OK, Mathew, what is the most difficult element of magic to master?' continued Professor Lucian.

'Black fire as an element has a mind and consciousness of its own,' Mathew replied.

'Well done! Now, Mithos, let's see if you can stay top of the class. Use the black flame in spell form.'

Mithos stood and walked to the front of the class, he clasped his hands together in order to focus his mana. (Mana is the key requirement for magic – the more mana a mage has the more powerful spells a mage could use).

He turned his right hand palm up, igniting a black flame. He ran his fingertips up the flame and covered his hand – it was controlled and ready to obey its master. The professor looked pleased, and began to speak to the class.

'Well done. It is clear that you have mastered the basics of that element well and since tomorrow is the weekend I will end class early today, but by Monday I want you all to have mastered every aspect of wind magic. On Monday I will test your powers with levitation by making you all levitate for a minimum of two minutes.'

He continued, 'Mithos, this book is for you. It teaches the ways to use the black flame and all of the spell forms, therefore I want you to be able to control fire completely within two weeks.'

Professor Lucian handed over the book, which was bound in red leather with a black flame on the cover. The title stuck in Mithos's mind, *The Book of Azumi.*

'Class dismissed,' Lucian declared. 'The training rooms on the third floor are reserved for the six of you all weekend.'

As the six students left the classroom Mithos already had the book open.

'Hey Mithos, want to get some coffee with 'us? Mithos looked up to see Mathew.

'Sorry but I'm going to study in the library for a while,' he replied

'You're always studying, Mithos, don't you ever have fun?' asked Nadia.

Mithos smiled, turned, and headed for the library.

'This is fun for me,' he said in answer to her question.

***

Mithos opened the big wooden doors. Most of the library was well organized and kept tidy, but one corner was a mess filled with towering columns of books, encasing another pile of books.

Mithos saw a small man searching the pile of books, as he did every day.

'Hey, Freddy! How are you today?' Mithos asked.

The man turned on first seeing Mithos, then jumped, startled, 'Oh, Mithos – it's you! Sorry, it's the colour of your eyes. Red is not all that common you know.'

Mithos smiled, 'Is my table available?'

A bigger man put down a heavy box filled with new books.

'Yeah since you always take it we permanently reserved it in your name,' the man said in a deep booming voice.

'Thanks, Dean,' Mithos said.

He sat at the reserved small table in the far corner. It was perfect for him, out of the way and secluded.

Studying the books before he tried to cast the spells suited him best, that way he could remember how much mana to use and the right forms to use – any error would mean his death.

Chapter Two

Officer Edwards, the commander of the school's combat mage guard, entered the headmaster's office.

'Headmaster, more people have gone missing and I think we have found the trail, but I would request your assistance, sir.'

The headmaster sat back in his chair, 'Are you sure the trail will lead to the one who has been doing all this? The one who is abducting our strongest Wizards?'

The officer stood nodding, 'Yes, sir, it is a fresh trail.'

The headmaster stood from his chair and removed his robes.

The headmaster, the chief officer and three other combat mages started to follow the trail. It led to a secret door hidden by grass in the teacher's garden, it led down a long staircase to a dark hallway.

'Headmaster what is this place? I have never seen it before.'

They walked down the hall and the headmaster disarmed a few traps that had been set for any trespassers.

'Headmaster, those traps … what level were they?' one of the combat mages asked.

'Only an expert could have set them like that,' he replied.

As they reached the door they could sense someone on the other side, so they took up positions; two either side of the door and one behind the headmaster. The combat mages drew their swords and the headmaster crossed his wrists, linked his hands to the door, and glanced to the two combat mages. They nodded.

The combat mages were ready and pulled the headmaster's hands from the door. It flew open and the two mages made their move; charging in with swords, soon followed by the headmaster. Before long the floor was covered in pools of blood, and strewn across was flesh cut from the attacker's bodies.

They heard a clink of metal and a scraping of bone coming from the far end of the dark room.

'Who's there?' one of the combat mages called. 'You, in the shadows! Come out!'

The headmaster waved his right hand in the air, lighting up the room as much as he could.

'Come out here right now and face your punishment!' the headmaster added.

They heard chuckling coming from the shadows, 'My, my, my,' said a sinister snake-like voice. 'And here I was, thinking I'd planned ahead by making traps to give me advanced warning.'

No matter how different it may have sounded, the headmaster couldn't forget that voice. The voice of the man he'd raised.

'Lucian? Please tell me it isn't you.'

The laugh got louder.

'And here I thought I could fool you by altering my vocal patterns, Headmaster.'

The figure came into the light, with no doubt it was Lucian. With a click of his fingers the room completely lit up, shedding a ghastly light on the room filled with bodies, some half dismembered.

'Why have you done this, lord Lucian?' the combat mage chief asked.

'Why not? Someone needs to create new magic so why not me?' he replied, smirking.

'But how does killing so many of your comrades help you create spells? What kind of twisted logic is that?'

Lucian's smile became cruel, as if he enjoyed their reaction.

'As you know, the basis of all magic is combining mana with a word or a gesture or even a simple thought – and I want to know it all. My research started with ways of giving the wielder a faster increase in mana, or faster ways of refilling the well we draw it from faster. These were successful but now I want more power, hotter fire, stronger wind … but I soon discovered that I would be dead before I could ever complete my research so I found ways to extend my life. What I want now is something on a far greater scale.'

'What forbidden magic are you searching for?' the headmaster asked.

'I will become a God, a living god, with eternal life and unparalleled power. I shall rule over this world bringing an end to war and murder for eternity. So tell me, what are a few dead mages compared to a world of peace?'

Without thinking one of the combat mages attacked, readying his sword for an overhead strike. Lucian smacked the palm of his hand just below the combat mage's navel and the mage crumpled to the ground holding his stomach.

Lucian smiled looking over his shoulder, 'Thank you for contributing to my research.'

They all watched as the combat mage held his stomach and rolled around in agony.

'What have you done Lucian?' the headmaster yelled.

Lucian looked over to the headmaster, 'Tell me, what do you think would happen if a strong gravitational pull was put in the centre of gravity of a human?'

The headmaster went white. They all knew what would happen.

'The gravitational pull I gave is slightly too strong for his body to take, I want to see every moment of this as he is slowly crushed by his own body.'

They all watched as the combat mage was forced into a ball, his screams cut short as his bone and blood scattered. Some of the blood sprayed on the other combat mage. How could he do it? How could he be so cruel as to implode someone and find it amusing? The other combat mage primed his sword and charged, not thinking, not paying attention to any order that was called out.

Lucian, with spread fingers, swiped his arm up and cast a burst of air that hit and stopped the combat mage from moving.

The headmaster watched in horror as the combat mage fell to the ground in five slices.

'You insane bastard!' the chief yelled. He built up energy and transferred it to his sword, then charged and spun sending a blue slash of energy at Lucian. He was already prepared and raised his shield, fizzling the energy out of the contact.

'Very good. I can see why you have your rank, but you shouldn't underestimate me.'

Lucian held out his right hand pulling the chief towards him. Lucian's hand was over his chest 'Dicone,' with that word a red circle appeared between Lucian's hand and the chief's chest, 'This is one of my creations with it I can suck out every drop of your mana such a shame you have to die for my research.' He couldn't hide his enjoyment draining the power and life from his victim.

The chief started to become thin and his skin dried up, as Lucian released the spell the chief dropped to the floor mummified. 'And then there was one. I never thought I would get to try my new power agents you so soon master.'

'No, you will die here before you can kill any more people,' Lucian took a combat position as if preparing for a fist fight the headmaster did the same they both charged throwing and blocking punches. The headmaster grabbed Lucian's wrist and threw him, Lucian rolled landing on his feet.

'So, Lucian, you remember the true essence of mage combat?'

Lucian smiled, 'Yes in order to conserve one's Mana a mage should use punches kicks and blades watching for an opening to use his magic or else have it thrown in his face.'

They clashed again dodging blocking and attacking seeing a blind spot, Lucian, unleashed a thin ray of energy but the headmaster dodged the attack and the beam put a small hole in the ground. The headmaster launched an energy spell of his own just missing Lucian as he sidestepped the attack.

'It would seem our skill at hand to hand combat is evenly matched but with magic we are at an impasse, this hall can't take too much damage if the magnitude of an explosion is too great it will collapse.'

Lucian turned his right palm up grasping his wrist with the left hand.

'Junok,' a purple ball appeared above his hand. Lucian threw the ball but the headmaster dodged it; as it hit one of the corpses it expanded to engulf the corpse then collapsed on itself removing the body from existence.

'Where did you learn that forbidden spell?'

'I have spent a lot of money and taken a lot of lives to gather relics that contained powerful magic with each of them I absorbed the knowledge of the spell or the mana sealed within. It has taken years but I am more than willing to go to any length. But there is one relic I am still searching for.'

'The pyramid of life, right? It doesn't exist.'

'I already have two pieces, and very soon I shall have the rest.'

The headmaster threw a blast of white light at Lucian; holding up his hand he brushed it aside; several other energy spells were launched, but each of them was sent away.

'Re'cole,' time started to slow as did the headmaster. Lucian started walking towards the headmaster; as he drew his sword he started to feel weak, he started to sweat, his legs and his sword felt heavy, then he remembered the spells the headmaster had used.

'You foolish old man, what have you done to me?' he lased the spells, Lucian gripped his sides from the pain. 'You stupid old fool, I will make you pay for this,' Lucian said, the pain evident in his voice. As he reached the door he lent up against the door frame. 'And just so you know – my experiments are already loose and I have my ways of keeping watch over them, good luck.' With those last words Lucian made his escape the headmaster heard the sounds of screaming yet more unfortunate victims.

'Sir down here more of them,' the headmaster awoke to the sound of clattering steel. 'Sir I've found the headmaster,' the room quickly filled with combat mages.

'Headmaster, what happened here?' The room was filled with the combat mages the four dead were removed as the medical team started treatment on the headmaster's wounds.

'Lucian has betrayed us,' the headmaster said; his voice was horse the words poured out like poison. Lucian was the Mage he raised since he was just a child.

Mithos couldn't find Lucian in his office. He would have to wait till Monday he decided to go to the student lounge on the third floor. The room was filled with students studying, the walls were covered with bookshelves, each book had spells potions or the rules that all mages should follow, the books were all spelled so that no one without the necessary skill or power could open or read them. As a high-ranking student, Mithos had no limit on what books he could read, the most dangerous books were kept in a room that was spelled for the advanced students, anyone else attempting to enter the room would first be warned of them, it would feel ice cold and if they tried to go further they would be rendered unconscious.

Mithos entered the advanced room, his classmates were already studying their chosen skills Mathew was a healer, his gift for healing injury was beyond that of any professor in the school. It was common for students to get injured during training so the medical mages would call on him for help. Mithos was skilled in combat, he was on a par with Lucian, however, his skill with fire was beyond Lucian's. Mithos took a book from the shelves it was one he only read in his spear time since his skill with fire magic was very advanced but there was always more to learn like how to use fire as a shield and he couldn't fully control the black fire yet.

The book he took from the shelf was but controlling the spell form and how to properly regulate the power for different spells simple ones such as the fire stream didn't require much just a steady stream of magic the more complex spells however could require a change in the amount of power used or they required a second spell to function. Andria was skilled at illusion magic her spells were extremely difficult to get out of, she once trapped Mithos in an illusion for two hours it was like his own personal hell he was surrounded by – screaming children and he hated loud shrieks.

Mithos found a paragraph on combining wind and fire magic with rotation control. As he was appointed to the combat mages he thought it best to learn what he could about all forms of magic; the more skilled you were the better the chance to be made an officer. Studying the spell forms Mithos realized how complex it would be. At the far end of the room was the practice area for the advanced students, the practice area had special safety features for fire spells, he need only use force magic to pull the lever and the door would drop stealing the air from the room taking the breath of life away from the flames.

On approach to the practice area Mithos held out his hand palm up igniting a fire ball he did the same with his left hand gathering air and creating a small air current using his mana the wind started to turn faster and faster when it became a small tornado he added the fire to the tornado. The fire turned faster till the fire had become the tornado. Mithos kept his right hand on top so he could contain the spell. Mathew looked up from his book.

'Mithos do we need to hide under the table again?' he asked.

'I don't think so,' Mithos replied somewhat hurt by his friend's lack of faith in his skill.

'Remember last time you had to repair the training area after your attempt at a lighting bomb spell,' Andria pointed out.

Mithos threw the swirling twisting fire to the practice area. He kept a steady stream of fire infused with his mana lowering or raising it when the spell began to waver. Mithos started to lose control of the fire tornado as it grew too much. Using his left hand Mithos threw a thin whip of force magic to the lever, the heavy, thick iron door slammed shut and soon enough the flame was snuffed out.

'What did I tell you, no need to worry,' he said. The door to the advanced students' room burst open, they all looked to the open door seeing a common student on his knees shivering. 'Did one of you just use a spell?'

'Yeeees,' Mithos said, curious of how this boy knew.

'Well I think the roof is on fire …'

Mithos went pale. As the other advanced students started to laugh Mithos ran to the common room seeing the flames he held up his hands, 'Vase'ta,' he yelled holding both his palms up, a huge burst of water drenched the ceiling. When he cut the water flow he sent pure mana untainted by elements of magic. As the magic wove inside the ceiling, the water started to dry and the scorch marks vanished, the flames didn't do too much damage so reversing the fire and water damage was rather quick and easy, much easier than completely rebuilding half a building.

With the damage repaired Mithos returned to the book where he found the mistake he had made in the spell, but the last time he used it the spell took a lot of his mana and repairing the ceiling took most of what he had spare.

In the early morning Mithos went to Lucian's office but he still wasn't there. It was not strange for Lucian to go on long trips over the weekend when the combat mages asked him to. Sometimes he would go somewhere for his own private study. Last time Lucian went on a trip he took Mithos with him, too, giving him experience in the real world, He learnt that combat mages would normally have to go on covert missions. It was difficult hiding the abilities he used every day. Mithos decided to relax for the day. A day without using magic that and a lot of food would help him regain the mana he had lost.

Mithos went to the dining hall. As always, the platters on the tables were full of hot food, one table held every type of meat from roast pork, bacon and sausages to lamb and steak. Another table held vegetables salads and roast vegetables. The third table was filled with tomato soup chicken soup and heavy broths.

Mithos grabbed a plate taking a huge piece of juicy pork with crackling he added a small pot of cockles and a lump of cheese with the vegetables he spooned on some garlic butter mushrooms and some fresh tomatoes. At the other end of the dining hall were huge tables each of them had places set and in front of each place was a silver jug and a chalice. He took a place where he would be alone putting his plate on the table. Mithos picked up the jug and whispered to it, 'Wine red.' The liquid poured out of the jugs was spelled so no matter what was in a jug you could change it for what you wanted. As Mithos started to tear in to the pork Mathew and Andria sat next to him.

'Mithos, could you be more barbaric, at least cut the meat,' Andria said.

He scowled at her, 'You try sleeping with no mana,' he replied with a mouth full of pork. Sara joined them looking at Andria's face then back to Mithos she rolled her eyes.

'You had better start cutting your meat, Mithos.'

He looked up from his plate, 'Mind your own business, I'm starving,' he said picking up a mushroom dripping with garlic butter. He looked at them and the strange faces they were pulling before popping it in his mouth. 'What's wrong?' he finally asked.

'Headmaster Strange is missing and the emergency room has been blocked off,' Mathew said.

'Professor Rohnal is also missing; they have most likely gone on a mission together they've done it before,' Mithos added as he took a sip of wine.

'Maybe you're right, but what about the emergency room.'

'The last time it was used was when someone came down with a contagious illness. There is no point in dwelling on it.'

After he finished his third helping Mithos grabbed a cup and the jug, 'Milk tea with sugar,' he whispered into it. He poured a hot cup of tea before he sat back in his chair. 'How are you guys doing with your studies,' he asked.

'Not bad, but could you help me with basic black flame control,' Mathew asked.

'Ask me tomorrow; right now I'm recharging my mana.'

Mithos spent half the day in his privet room resting reading one of his favourite books it was a story Lucian read to him as a child about the legendary shadow reapers they were creatures who looked human but had no emotion but the story told of a male and female shadow reaper who fell in love and how they fought for their right to love, and were inevitably executed but as a sign of respect they were buried together it was tragic with a nice end as their spirits were reunited in the spirit world. Lucian told him lots of stories since he was left at the school when he was two years old Lucian raised him with little help from the other professors he still considered Lucian as his father he couldn't wait till Monday when he could ask Lucian for advice on how to control the fire tornado better.

Andria entered Mithos's room without knocking, 'You do realize I could have been naked, right?' he said with a wink.

'I'm sure it would be the same as walking in on a woman,' she said with a mischievous grin. As he stood she wrapped her arms around his neck as she gave him a deep kiss she felt warm her lips were soft as velvet. She pulled away slightly and took in a gasp of oxygen.

'Wow and that was just your hello, how do you say you love someone?' Mithos asked.

She gave him a slight grin as she put her hand down his trousers and kissed him again. She pulled away again pushing him to the bed.

'Do you want the full confession?'

He returned the smile as she laid on top of him kissing him deep rolling them over Mithos blew out the candle.

Chapter Three

Headmaster Strange awoke to find himself in the emergency room it appeared to be sealed off from the school; looking around he saw combat mages at every entrance and at the windows. The deputy commander of the combat mages was in the chair next to his bed.

'Headmaster, you're awake.'

The headmaster sat up in the hospital bed. 'Yes, how long have I been here?'

'Two days, headmaster; I must ask what did you say about Lucian?'

Headmaster Strange felt tears fall from his eyes.

'The people who have gone missing they were murdered by Lucian.'

Neither of them spoke for a while they heard the combat mage outside the door shift from one foot to the other having being standing in one place for the last two days.

'Lucian experimented on them alive and dead.'

'What is our next move, sir?'

Headmaster Strange looked out the window, seeing the sun about to rise – it was very early.

'I will eat then call all the students and teachers to the assembly hall; give them two hours before calling them.' The deputy commander saluted and left the emergency room to fetch some food. Mithos lay in bed stroking Andria's long blonde hair, her hand was rested on his chest.

'Guess I was wrong about the woman thing,' she said still panting from the exertion of the night's activity. Mithos kissed her ruby lips. As they separated, the door swung open, Mithos raised a shield over the door to prevent any entry. They saw Mathew standing there.

'Oh for god's sake, will you two love birds hurry up and get dressed, all students have been summoned to the assembly hall.' As Mathew walked away Mithos let loose a small stream of Force to close the door.

They got out of bed and started to dress, their skin-tight white trousers creased and the red tunics crinkled, they looked like they had slept in their uniforms, they got their boots on and grabbed their basket swords running for the hallway, fixing their swords as they ran. They finally reached the other third year students. As he was ranked number one of the advanced students it was Mithos's duty to command the third years. Mithos reached the front of the students, he drew his sword, 'Forward march!' he yelled. He led them down from the third floor of the student quarters they marched across the courtyard the garden was beautiful in the early morning sun. When they reached the main building one of the teachers was waiting for them.

'Advanced student at the front of the hall, the rest of you follow me,' he said.

Mithos led the other students to the chairs in front of where the third years stood. The room was live with gossip. Mithos was able to hear some of it; seemed to be about the disappearance of mages both students and teachers. On the stage the teachers sat in carved seats, each of the chairs had carvings relating to the subject they taught. Lucian's seat was empty now, it was getting strange, Lucian never spent this long on a mission outside of holidays.

Headmaster Strange approached the pedestal the room fell to complete silence.

'We have found out the cause of the disappearances. The students and teachers who went missing were murdered.'

The room burst with renewed chattering. The headmaster shot a glance to Mithos and the other advanced students. They all stood bringing the room to silence. With the students quiet the advanced students sat back down again.

'The murderer was experimenting on them, searching for forbidden magics.'

'Who was it?' a student yelled.

'Lucian Rohnal, he managed to escape killing four combat mages and wounding me' once again the students started to talk. Mithos angry about what he heard, stood and waved his right hand, stealing the sound from the other students.

'Keep quiet and I will return your voices.'

The students covered their mouths nodding to say they understood. Mithos clicked his fingers and sat back down. Andria put her hand on his, locking their fingers together. Headmaster Strange continued with his speech

'Lucian Rohnal is now an enemy, a rouge mage. A level ten warrant is now on his head, will the students he taught please stand.' All eight of them stood. 'Follow the combat mage to the interrogation room for questioning.'

Mithos stood and led the others to the combat mage at the back of the room. The interrogation room had ten chairs, each of them took a seat, the room was mostly dark the only light given off came from the four torches on the walls. They sat in silence till the door opened again when headmaster Strange entered the room

'Did any of you notice anything strange about Lucian before today?' They all shook their heads 'So he didn't seem to give of a hint of something different in the way he spoke or acted?'

'No,' they all said as one.

Headmaster Strange sat opposite them. 'I'm sorry, I know how difficult it must be for you all, especially you, Mithos, since he raised you and like you he was abandoned at our doorstep.'

They sat in silence for a while as the women whipped tears from their eyes.

'For now none of you will have a teacher since there is no point in slowing your studies, but since the eight of you know him and his power best I will arrange for you to be attached to a combat mage squad.'

Mithos sat in his room after the chat in the interrogation room. As far as he knew the others were most likely doing the same but what occupied his mind were questions; why would Lucian betray them, the man whose name he shared, his teacher and the closest thing he had to a father?

Mithos's bedroom door opened, Andria walked in and sat on the bed next to him.

'Still upset, are you?' she asked as she put an arm around him.

'What gave it away?' he asked. 'I am more angry than upset.'

She cupped his cheek turning him to face her. 'Don't compare yourself to him.'

'How did you know I was …?'

'He raised you and taught you, but you are different people.'

He stared in to her eyes remembering how he fell in love with her, she leaned forward and kissed his forehead. Mithos pulled her to his embrace; he felt safe in her arms. Mathew and Nala stood pacing outside Mithos's room they both knew what Lucian meant to Mithos. They arrived with Andria but she convinced them to let her go in first. After fifteen minutes they got tired of waiting and Nala opened the door. They saw Andria and Mithos sitting on the bed in each other's embrace.

'Finished the fun already?' Nala joked. She always had the talent to making the worst joke at the worst time, but making them all laugh anyway. With Mathew pulling his arm they got Mithos out of his room dragging him to the private training area. The chairs and tables were all facing the same way towards the far wall. There was a chalkboard in the centre of the wall and to each side were bookcases. Mathew dragged Mithos to the far side. 'Why am I here what do you all want?'

'Lucian is too strong for us since there is no one who can teach us we want you to teach us combat magic,' Andria said.

He looked around at the bookshelves, everything he knew came from these books they knew this so why did they ask him for help?

'There is little I could teach you; I can tell you to read those books,' he pointed at the book shelf on the right wall, he knew he could tell them the best books to read, but that would be as far as he could go with teaching and if he was to be the one who captured or killed Lucian he had training to do.

Under his direction they took the books they would need, the few books left were the ones he had not read Mithos pointed to a table in the corner of the room and told them that it was for him to study on, they all knew that he liked to study alone and that he couldn't learn otherwise. Reading the books Mithos realized that it would do no good Lucian knew forbidden magic. 'This is useless,' he yelled throwing the book he was reading.

'What do you mean?' Mathew asked.

'Lucian knows every spell in every book. He wrote some of them with spells he created from his twisted experiments.'

They all looked down at their books they understood what he meant, they all felt the same about it, they didn't stand a chance with their current powers even if they were all to attack him Lucian would kill them in an instant. Mithos thought for a while on how to gain the power needed to fight Lucian or at least to survive a fight with him, it came to him, Headmaster Strange he should know a couple of books that could help. Mithos stood and left the third floor of the students' dorm. The sunny day had turned to a bright rainy day the sky looked all the more beautiful for it. Mithos reached a huge marble building, the area set aside for the teachers, the door was bigger than the one for the students. Around the arch were ornate carvings in an ancient language that was said to be the language of the shadow reapers. Mithos let a flow of power come through the palm of his hand as he placed it on the door it was the only way for the teachers to know he wanted to see someone it was Headmaster Strange who opened the door.

'Ah Mithos Rohnal; come to see me, my boy?' the headmaster asked Mithos gave a bow of his head showing his respect.

'Yes, sir, I want to know is there a spell that could help protect me from Lucian or any other mage who would kill me?' he asked. The headmaster's eyebrows went up as if weighing his options then a slight smile came to his lips.

'About time one of you came to me for this.'

Mithos couldn't believe it. The headmaster wouldn't offer the help, they had to ask for it.

'What can we learn?'

'Not we, you, you came to me you asked for the help, until the others come and ask they must not know about this,' the headmaster said.

Mithos was taken to the teachers' offices down to the basement headmaster Strange picked up a ring bearing a strange symbol he offered it to Mithos.

'Take it as a gift.'

Mithos saw the same ring on the headmaster's hand.

'What is it for?' Mithos asked.

'It marks you as a Warlock one of the elite.'

Mithos had heard of the warlock order, but not of what they did. 'What does it mean to be a warlock?'

'Take the ring and I will tell you.'

Mithos took the ring and put it on the middle finger on his right hand the sword in the centre of the ring covered his knuckle, around the outside were lined symbols each meant something different it was the same language as the words over the arch of every door in the teachers' offices.

'The warlocks are chosen to be warriors against evil we are agents who work to bring an end to the evil use of magic. By taking the ring you are an agent that can be used to kill evil men and mages; some of them will be students at this school.' Headmaster Strange took Mithos to the back room. Unlike the main basement it was well lit revealing every inch of the room. It was built for one on one teaching, the walls of the room were filled with bookshelves, in the centre of the room was a desk and two chairs.

'Take a seat, Mithos.' As Mithos sat down the headmaster picked a book from one of the shelves and sat down opposite him. 'The best way to protect yourself is through defence shields using the raw force of magic to create a perfect shell for long or short periods of time, and you must develop the skill to make a perfect shell in a split second any crack in battle will be your death.' Mithos thought it a simple matter but then he thought better arrogance destroys the footholds of victory. 'Read this book when you are done I will demonstrate how a shield should be.'

The book was bound in brown leather with silver lettering on the cover he started reading. The book went into great detail on the spell form of a simple shield how it should work in waves to breakdown small spells half way through the book it went to detail on a full body shield including the math of how much mana to use in the constant mana different spells require a different strength of shield. If the shield was too weak to conserve mana it wouldn't work, but if it was too strong it could deflect most spells but at a cost of mana leading to the inability to use any spell form. When Mithos finally closed the book the headmaster looked at him.

'What do you think?' he asked.

'It will take a while before I can create one ready for battle,' he thought for a while. 'Lucian can create shields, can't he?' The headmaster just nodded. 'How powerful is he?' Mithos had finally asked the question the headmaster was waiting for.

'If I didn't know how to lace my attacking spells with a weakening spell he would have killed me.' Mithos swallowed at being told about what Lucian did in his secret lab, at the powers he displayed when he killed the four combat mages. He felt sick at the gruesome detail Headmaster Strange went into in describing what happened. Headmaster Strange stood telling Mithos to use an attacking form on him. Mithos threw a fireball at him as the headmaster held out his hand the fire dispersed on closer inspection the air around his hand looked wavy like it would in the desert heat he saw how the small shield was to be used using wind and fire magic. He launched a stronger attack. Headmaster Strange raised his other hand as the attack engulfed the headmaster it, too, was dispersed. Rippling air surrounded him, that was the shell the headmaster was talking about. Mithos was able to master the small shield in a short amount of time, but a full body shield would be more difficult. Headmaster Strange used a stronger spell. Mithos threw up the full body shield, but it shattered on contact with the spell.

'Warlocks normally face more than one enemy that use stronger magic than this. If you were to be sent out tomorrow with your current abilities, you would die.' After a little more training and many failed attempts Headmaster Strange called it a day and said they would continue tomorrow. Mithos was ordered to never take off the ring he walked around the school knowing what Lucian would do if he came back. He would lay waste to the school. Mithos eventually found his way back to the third floor dorm as he entered his room it was empty all of his belongings were gone and the bed had been stripped. The door behind him opened, it was Professor Neco Smith.

'Ah, Mithos, you have been moved to Lucian's old house.'

Mithos looked at him, 'Why am I being moved, sir?'

He walked closer to Mithos. 'Warlocks cannot stay with other students.' He escorted Mithos to one of the cottages near the wall. They walked to the third cottage, there was a man standing outside. As they got close enough Mithos saw Siren, a fourth year advanced student, his hair was slicked back blond, his eyes were different colours – the left was green the right was blue. As they stopped they saw his twin sister, Sireen. Her hair was blonde and shoulder length, her eyes were also blue and green, but the other way around.

'Why are you here, Siren?' Mithos asked. He smiled showing off the ring on his right hand as he opened the door.

Sireen smiled showing the ring on her right hand; around the school there was no man or woman who didn't know their names they were seen as the objects of pure lust every man wanted to spend one night with Sireen and every woman wanted her brother in the same way.

The way they acted, though, earned them the nickname – the Incest Twins – it seemed to most like they wanted to be with each other and no one else, but Mithos knew different, since Sireen was his first girlfriend and the first girl he slept with and Andria hated that fact. Sireen showed him in to the house when Professor Smith left them.

There were three rooms; a kitchen, a dining room and a living room. Sireen seemed very happy to see him.

'Well, Mithos, come to have some fun, from what I remember you were very fun,' she said with a mischievous grin. She was as seductive as ever.

'None of that, sis, leave the poor boy alone. Andria won't be happy if she hears about it.'

Sireen showed Mithos to his room. It was bigger than it looked. The book shelf held more books than he remembered. His spare uniform was in the open wardrobe, the red coat was on the wooden torso in the far corner, the window let in a lot of light. He saw to the right of the room a mannequin with knee high black leather boots, black leather trousers and a black cotton long sleeved t-shirt. The black vambraces held the symbol of the warlock, there was a black leather tabard that came down to the knees and around the shoulders was a black hooded cloak held in place with a silver broach with the warlock's sword.

'That is your new uniform put it on we need to leave soon,' Sireen said.

'Where are we going?' Mithos asked.

'Headmaster has called us to a meeting all members of the order of warlocks, just hurry.' The uniform fit him perfectly like a tailor had measured him in his sleep everything was clean, the leather had a shine so did the buckles running down the sides of the boots. Putting on the cloak he ran downstairs, the tabard was kept in place with a leather belt, the cloak billowed out with the breeze that came in through the open window.

Chapter Four

Lucian reached the tower he had been travelling for almost a week as he approached the tower the door opened for him. A red trench coat with black flames embroidered materialized as if from thin air; the two men bowed on his approach.

'Lord Lucian, welcome back,' they said as he walked passed them without responding or a giving them a second look.

The tower was part of the puzzle for him gaining absolute power. It was a taller than most castles. It was ancient, older than memory. Reaching the top of the tower, Lucian entered the throne room, he was met by his students, his true students, the ones he taught everything to. He chose them because of the special powers they held, powers that hadn't been seen in thousands of years. In the centre of the room was a man with his hands bound.

'Is this the one?' he asked.

'Yes, my lord, he knows of the towers,' Pain answered. He was skilled at making people suffer; his deep voice made him seem dominant over all the other students leant against the wall.

'You tell Master Rohnal what you know about how the tower works.'

The man was covered with cuts, his face was covered with boils, some that had burst judging by the yellow colour of the puss leaking from the open wounds. It was Pain who gave them to him.

'Pain, we don't want him dead from the infection.'

'He won't die, but I will remove the infection when he tells us what we want to know. It is only through pain that we understand each other. It is the only way we can get the truth.'

Lucian stood by the throne he didn't dare sit on it, not knowing what would happen. He watched as Pain went to work earning his name, the man's screams could travel for miles. Eventually the man surrendered what they wanted between gasps and screams.

'The one who sits on the throne becomes master of the tower. From then on joining the tower gives you the rest.'

Pain looked up smiling at finally getting the information. Lucian thought to reward him, he gave Pain a grin and a nod. Pain attended to the prisoner, waving his hand over the man's face. The boils and open wounds had gone the agony, too, had gone. He stepped back pointing the palm of his hand to the man.

'Know pain feel pain understand pain and you shall know life, now you will know life.'

The man started to scream again, his shredded cloths started to evaporate, followed by his skin. The air was thick with a red mist as the man's skin, muscles, veins, arteries and organs all turned to dust. The screams stopped when the flesh was gone. Lucian loved to watch Pain work even more then he liked to watch his second in command Death. Lucian approached the throne and took the seat it started to change form. The tower gave him the knowledge he sought. It showed five towers. The one at the centre was glowing red, the one he now owned. The other four had power requirements: a user of Pain in command and a sacrifice of eight hundred souls, a user of

Fear and a sacrifice of four hundred souls, a user of Death and a sacrifice of one thousand souls, the final one required a master of Shadow and the sacrifice of his soul.

Lucian wouldn't be able to continue his search whilst the combat mages were looking for him, it was something to be dealt with along with other matters he would have to make contact with his spies soon.

Mithos was guided by the twins around the school to the meeting place. They all had their hoods up so no one would recognize them, they had their swords at their hips keeping their hands on the hilts of the swords as they made their way through the school grounds. They saw several others in the same uniforms.

'Why have I never seen you heading to meetings before?' Mithos asked.

'We have never been summoned before curfew it normally means bounty hunting is involved. You are new so I will tell you how it works, we operate in teams of three. Lucian was a member of our team, we noticed him acting strange so we informed the headmaster about it.'

'And the bounties?' Mithos asked.

'They are up for bidding each team takes a bounty based on the abilities of the weakest member the payment is split evenly between us.'

Mithos absorbed everything Siren had told him as he, Sireen, Siren and the other warlocks made their way through the school grounds. The third year council rep approached them. The advanced students had no intention on being class rep they thought it was a waste of time. The rep stopped in front of them.

'Who are you? Let me see your student ID or your access pass.'

Mithos stopped Siren and Sireen, thinking they might harm the rep. Instead Mithos approached the rep as he started to talk again. Mithos waved his index and middle fingers in front of the rep's mouth stealing his voice. It was a simple spell, but Mithos knew the rep and knew he didn't know how to break the spell.

'Brother, you don't need to do that just push it aside and let's be on our way,' Siren said with a small grin on his lips.

'But this thing needs to learn to hold his tongue so I will leave him like this for the day. I will remove it later.'

Mithos pushed passed the student rep, the other two followed close behind him. They reached the location of the meeting there were at least nine teams there on the stage stood the headmaster wearing much the same, but the silver items they wore were gold on him and a gold medallion around his neck.

'There are twenty contracts all, assassinations the highest price is on Lucian Rohnal. Nine thousand gold pieces, this is an open contract for anyone who finds him.'

The headmaster went through all contracts one by one. Siren took one contract Sireen took another they were the lowest price contracts the headmaster offered. The second highest no one wanted to take it. Mithos put his hand up to take the dangerous assignment Siren tried to stop him, but he wanted it so she would not be able to stop him from this path.

'Why do you want that contract you are too weak to beat him?' she asked.

'It will be my test to see how far from Lucian I am,' he said with determination.

Neither of them could stop him from taking this path. They set out for the first contract all they had to do was kill the target and from what the wanted poster said Moran'ak was a bandit who used stolen magic to target wandering traders. Stolen magic was the lifeblood of a dead mage; the last spell the mage used made an imprint in the blood turning it to a magic potion ready to bottle and use. They got horses from the school stable. Mithos took a black stallion, Siren took a beige mare, Sireen took the brown horse. It wasn't a long trip to the ruin where the bandits made camp, but they would have to be careful since they used stolen magic and they could have laid traps. As night came they reached the ruin they could see fires in the ruin. They heard laughter, the bandits seemed to be celebrating something. Mithos and the twins dismounted deciding to sneak up on them. They didn't encounter any type of alarm or trap as they got closer Siren gave them a sign to draw their swords Sireen and Mithos followed his lead. He gave them a count on his fingers three two one. When Siren clenched his fist they jumped over the partly destroyed wall striking down the three bandits with their swords the others jumped at the sound of steel ripping through bone. Mithos saw the target reach for a bottle. Mithos threw a blast of flame to some of the bandits. Siren started running for the target. Moran'ak started to run. Sireen was busy fighting off some of the other bandits. Finishing with his five, Mithos was going to try and help Sireen.

'No help Siren, the target is all that matters,' she said.

Mithos nodded and started running to Siren as he came into view Mithos saw Siren dip his fingertips in a small pool of water. Mithos saw Siren lift his hand with the middle finger held down with his thumb. Mithos heard Siren utter an incantation before he flicked his finger. Soon after, Moran'ak collapsed to the floor. When they caught up to the fallen man Siren still held out his hand. Mithos saw it was water drops on Siren's finger. Since it was an assassination mission, Siren flicked his middle finger firing a drop of water through the man's heart. Mithos severed the man's head as proof. Siren assured him it wasn't necessary, but he took it any way.

They rode back to the school. It was only three hours from the ruin to the school, they knew the headmaster wouldn't have gone to sleep yet. They went to the teachers' building and Mithos holding the bag holding the head placed his right hand on the door, but it opened before he could push it opened. Professor Smith opened the door and he jumped back a bit at seeing them in their black cloaks. Mithos found it funny.

'Oh you're warlocks; come in.' He took them to the teachers' lounge where they saw the headmaster sitting alone at a table. He looked up as they approached. Mithos dumped the bag on the table and Headmaster strange opened it and saw the head of the bandit, Moran'ak.

'You didn't need to bring back the head just a little blood, but you did well for your first assignment, Mithos.' He tossed a coin purse to them. 'Three hundred gold as promised, you should get some rest.'

Before they left through the door he called out to them.

'Mithos, lessons tomorrow morning, don't forget.'

They took off their hoods when they reached their cottage. As Siren and Sireen sat in the living room, Mithos sent a little flame from his finger to the wood in the fireplace. It was a cold night. Mithos was thankful for the warmth of his cloak. When he reached the table, Mithos saw three piles of gold.

'One hundred each. Mithos, that pile is yours.' Siren pointed to the pile of gold in the centre of the table, there was a black coin purse on top of the pile. Mithos tipped the coins into the purse. As Mithos and Siren were talking in the living room Sireen brought in a pot of tea with three cups she poured three cups of tea whilst Mithos hung up the cloaks. Mithos Siren and Sireen were drinking tea when they heard a knock at the door. Mithos went to answer the door. It was Andria Mathew and Sara; they stared at him. He realized he was still in his warlock's uniform, but since they wouldn't know what it meant he paid no attention to it.

'Hi, what's up?' Mithos asked.

'Why have you been moved here? We looked in your room but it was completely empty.'

Before he could answer Sireen appeared behind him.

'What's going on, Mithos?' she asked.

He was right when he thought Andria wouldn't be happy knowing Sireen was living with him they all knew that Sireen was his first girlfriend, the fact that she looked like lust in flesh made it worse. Andria saw that Mithos and Sireen were wearing the same outfit.

'Why is she here?' Andria hissed.

'And why are you dressed like that?' Mathew added.

It all brought Siren to the door.

'Mithos, invite them in,' Siren said. He seemed a little calmer than his sister about the situation. With them all sat down Siren sent Sireen to get extra cups. Mathew clocked the cloaks hanging on the wall, he was the first to break the silence.

'So you three were with the people dressed in black we saw earlier?'

Mithos wasn't surprised that they would figure it out, the hooded cloaks hid their faces, but not the rest of the uniform.

'Yes, we were with them,' Siren said before Mithos could. Mithos figured that since Siren had been a warlock for so long he would know what they could and could not say then again Mithos didn't think they would be allowed to admit to it. Siren saw what he was thinking.

'If they figure it out, Mithos, then we are allowed to tell them what we are and what we do, but not the way to join.'

As Sireen came back with three extra cups and a full pot of tea Andria just stared at her making them all more than a little uncomfortable. Once again Mathew broke the silence.

'So, Mithos, what do warlocks do?'

Siren took a sip of tea, 'We cannot tell you that I'm sorry.'

Mathew seemed annoyed when the silence returned Mithos just wanted the visit to be over. He couldn't take the look Andria was giving him. They stayed for an hour before Sara saw how Mithos was fidgeting.

'Well we had better go,' she gripped Andria's shoulder and whispered to her, 'before we wear out our welcome.'

Andria stood and headed for the door with Sara and Mathew in tow. They opened the door to see the headmaster weighting for them. Sara and Mathew backed off. This was only the second time they had come face to face with Headmaster Strange. He cast an intimidating shadow.

'Going somewhere?' he said raising an eyebrow. Before they could answer he cut them off. 'Of course not, at least not till I have spoken to you.'

Mithos held out his hand in invitation. The headmaster entered the house and sat at the armchair next to the fireplace. Sireen fetched a cup so she could pour the headmaster a cup of tea. Mithos and Siren took the other chairs, Mathew Sara and Andria stood behind them. When Sireen returned the two men stood, all three stood to attention with their left hands on their swords. They dropped to a knee putting the index and middle finger of their right hand to their foreheads. They chanted as one; 'Honoured elder, our swords for your weapon, our lives as your shield, our power at your command.' The headmaster smiled.

'Thank you, my children, be at your ease.'

Mithos and Siren returned to their chairs. Sireen took one of the dining room chairs sitting next to the two warlocks.

'Mithos I need you to take Andria Sara and Mathew on a mission tomorrow afternoon.' Siren and Sireen looked confused, but they would since Mithos was new to the warlocks.

'I'm sending you to a place where Lucian has been conducting his experiments, at least that is what my contacts say.' He turned to the siblings, 'You two will have to work as a team of two for now.' The headmaster took a sip of tea as the others sat and stood speechless unable to bring any question to words. After a couple of minutes of silence Mithos finally spoke.

'Elder, what should we do if we find Lucian there?'

The headmaster put down his empty cup. 'You will return and report your findings to me.'

'Yes, elder, I understand.'

Headmaster Strange stood, 'Then I will take my leave. After your lesson you will lead them on the mission.'

As the headmaster left Mithos pulled Andria to his embrace. 'See you tomorrow, my love,' he said before kissing her lips. She flashed him a smile, her fears of him and Sireen living under the same roof put to rest. She headed back to the students' dorms.

***

Lucian sat on his new throne holding a Vol'mat. The Vol'mat is a purple crystal that possesses the ability to communicate over long distances.

'What do you have for me?' Lucian asked.

'Mithos has joined the warlocks, my lord,' the voice replied. Lucian smiled from hearing the news.

'He seems to be developing well. How are his powers progressing?' Lucian asked anxious for the news on his experiment.

'His powers are still growing, my lord, though he still favours the fire element.'

The news of Mithos's success was music to his ears.

'Keep watching him and inform me of his movements.'

'Yes, my lord,' the voice replied.

The Vol'mat lost its purple glow turning to a regular stone as the magical connection was lost. Lucian beckoned Death to come forward he went to a knee bowing his head to Lucian.

'My lord, do you have a mission for me?' he asked head still bowed.

'Yes, my friend, I do. It is almost time for us to make our move. If the school isn't taken care of soon they will become a problem later on. Gather our forces; in five days we attack.'

Death smiled at the order since he lived for the sole purpose of killing.

'Yes, my lord, it shall be done.'

Clicking his fingers he vanished into the shadows.

Slowly Lucian's plans were coming together. His favourite test subject was advancing at the right pace and the mages had no idea what plans he laid for them. It was all going so well.

'My lord I have received information that Mithos is to lead a mission to one of your deserted laboratories,' the voice came from the shadow in the far corner of the room.

'Which one?' Lucian asked as he looked at the map on the table in front of his throne.

'The lab in Azura, my lord.' Lucian turned to the shadow.

'Then I will just have to send my old student a present it's only fair.'

Lucian raised his left hand it was a signal to his generals to form two ranks with the throne in the centre. Lucian paced between the two lines looking from one general to the other.

'I need someone to give Mithos a true test I want you to attack him when he reaches the lab any volunteers?'

They all put their hands up enthusiastically Lucian continued looking, gauging their powers.

'Most of you would kill him.' He pointed to the only general with his red hood up. 'You on the other hand, General Vincent Licough, you will follow my orders to the letter.' The general bowed.

'And what are your orders, my lord?' Lucian smiled this would be perfect. 'Fight Mithos, but don't kill him. His friends, though, are yours to play with.'

Chapter Five

Mithos went downstairs to the dining room. He heard a noise coming from the kitchen.

'Mithos that you?'

Mithos was relieved to hear Sirens voice. 'Yeah, morning, Siren, how are you today?'

Siren brought in a tray holding a pot of tea and three cups and placed them on the table. Mithos and Siren decided to talk whilst they drank their tea.

'Be careful on this mission and if you run into Lucian run don't even try to fight him just run.'

Mithos turned to face Siren dropping his cup. 'How can you ask me to do that? How can I run, Siren, when I know what he has done?' Mithos asked with anger heating his voice. 'Because if you try to kill him you will die. Like the headmaster said – Lucian is too strong and he can and will kill you if he sees you. So be smart and protect the others.'

They both stopped talking as they heard the floorboards creak. As they looked at the dining room door Mithos's jaw dropped.

'What are you doing, Sireen, did you forget Mithos is living here now?' Siren yelled. She was wearing nothing but her underwear Mithos's gaze jumped all over her body pausing at every perfect curve but his main focus was pulled to her cleavage and the bra did little to conceal the sheer size of her breasts. He was almost overwhelmed by the pure lust building inside him. Why was that, he thought, he had seen her naked before, they had had sex when they were a couple, he guessed it was more because she was more developed over these two years. Sireen looked around confused she finally looked down but she only shrugged which just seemed to make Siren more irritated.

'Sireen go upstairs and put some clothes on or I will drag you up and dress you like when we were kids.'

The suggestion made her smile; as it grew so too did the intense red on Siren's cheeks. Ten minutes of the twins yelling seemed like ten hours between Siren telling her to get dressed and Sireen protesting that she wasn't ashamed of her body. She finally stormed upstairs to get some clothes on. Mithos felt like he would overheat since in her argument she got close to him resting her breasts on his back asking if he had a problem with her body. Mithos drew the short straw to cook breakfast so he got started whilst they were waiting for Sireen to get dressed. So he lit the cooking hearth putting a pan over the heat, Mithos grabbed some sausages bacon tomatoes and eggs. As Mithos was cooking, Siren kept the teapot full siren came down in her mages robes sky blue with silver trim around the cuffs and collar, Mithos was the only one in the black warlock outfit. Sireen chose the right time to come down Mithos was just dishing out the breakfast. Siren got the table ready when the last was plated they all sat at the small dinner table to eat. No matter how lewd she was in the mornings at the dinner table Sireen was pure elegance. Siren on the other hand was a messy eater he was fast, too, leading him to spray Mithos and Sireen Mithos couldn't help but think he just wanted to get the washing up out of the way he could almost swear if there was a god for fast eaters Siren would be chosen for the job.

Mithos met the headmaster at the training spot inside the teachers building he was ready and eager to learn Mithos stood in the centre of the room so they could continue their lesson on shields.

'I will throw different spells at you, use small shields to disperse the magic.'

Mithos stood in place. The only light was on him as the headmaster moved around in the shadows.

'Don't rely on your eyes they can deceive you. Feel out the mana.' Mithos nodded as he tried to feel it. As the first spell came for him, Mithos froze the ball of red static energy and it moved slowly. But Mithos was leaving it for too long, just before the spell hit Mithos threw up a small shield. The spell broke in his palm the excess energy severed his fingertips causing him to scream in pain as blood gushed from the open wounds.

'That shield would be your death against Lucian.' The headmaster returned Mithos's fingertips, but he left the pain as a lesson. Lucian would be cruel and cut him to pieces. Another red ball of static energy came for Mithos; his head was filled with thoughts on what would happen if he faced Lucian in this state. Headmaster Strange watched as his spell came too close to Mithos the sudden vibration of a shield appeared in the small of his back it didn't break the spell it devoured the mana powering the spell.

'The draining shield when did he learn that?' The headmaster whispered. He threw a more powerful spell and increased the speed it was the same thing – no shell, just the vibration then nothing – the mana powering that spell was absorbed. Headmaster Strange threw a stronger spell, one made to kill. It was too fast to dodge, Mithos had to defend the vibration of his shield returned to cover him as it scanned he mana it told Mithos that the attacking spell couldn't be absorbed since it was in the shape of a blade not a blast. To combat the blade Mithos added a rotation to the shield. When the spell impacted the shield the rotation worked as a sling shot to send the spell back at the headmaster. Mithos was facing him. His eyes turned a dark red powered by rage.

'Who are you?' the headmaster asked. He knew it wasn't Mithos. The other smiled.

'I am Mithos, Horatio Strange, that last spell was supposed to kill, right?' Mithos's aura changed from the calm green to pure black. A sinister smile grew on his lips.

'So you are the result of Lucian's experiment, am I correct?'

The evil grin grew with a snigger. 'Yes I am,' it said with a deep double voice.

'It is a strange experiment, splitting Mithos's mind. The Mithos you know should be a lot stronger, but you already knew that.'

'What gave it away Horatio?' the other Mithos asked.

'Mithos is covered in a spell form entwined with his vital organs. If I were to disconnect them he would die, but tell me, we found several mages dead outside the grounds, but Lucian didn't do it.'

Mithos laughed thinking of them. 'There were twenty of them sent by Lucian to attack Mithos, so I took over his body and dealt with them, it was Lucian's form of a test.'

Before the other Mithos could go on the headmaster launched an attack meant to help diffuse spell forms, but Mithos blew a puff of air infused with hidden mana sending the spell flying back. The spell form was changed to a lethal wave of pure energy. The headmaster dodged the spell. Returning fire he threw up his hands, the air around Mithos crackled as the air exploded with mana the explosions that were too close to him were confined by imprisonment shields, they were spells Mithos shouldn't be able to know.

'I know what you are thinking, Horatio, how does he know such powerful spells when he's only a third year?' The other Mithos threw up his hands changing from defence to attack; he launched a barrage of wind blade spell forms each cutting the ground where the headmaster was. They would have all hit him if he was just a little slower. Mithos stopped his next attack

'Damn, thought I would have more time.' He looked back at the headmaster. 'Make sure you raise my other half well. Without our power Lucian will win.' The sinister smile returned. 'And don't tell Mithos about me or the spell form – he is not ready for that.'

'How do you know so many high-level spells?'

'Mithos has read every book available to students, but the knowledge came to me. He was even able to sneak into the sixth years' rooms without damaging the shields. He really is a smart one. I do have a little advice for the mission today. Have three sixth year Warlocks shadow them just in case.'

Before the headmaster could say anything else Mithos collapsed. Mithos awoke to find himself in a wooden chair he looked around the room and saw the headmaster opposite him and sitting in the chairs were the twins.

'Ah you are finally awake the. Shield you put up was too strong for the attack and you passed out.' Even with what the other Mithos said there was no way he could tell his student that he was one of Lucian's experiments. 'You had better get going, your mission starts soon; the others are waiting for you.'

Mithos grabbed his black hooded cloak and left the teachers' building. He met Mathew, Sara, Andria and Gilbert by the front gate with Professor Murray.

'OK, the mission is recon only don't engage the enemy unless you have no other choice is that understood?' the professor asked, emphasizing the point.

'Yes, sir,' they answered as one.

'Mithos you will be team leader.'

'Yes, sir,' Mithos said standing tall.

'Good luck, come back safe.'

Mithos gave a nod before setting off.

'How long will it take us Mithos?' Mathew asked.

'There is a small town just on the other side of the Brak'stell River. We will be there in just over a day. We should be able to get some horses there.' he said not slowing his pace. 'But we are going through regal forest; that is where we set the horses loose. Then the fog marsh.'

'But wouldn't it be better over the mountains?' Sara pointed out.

'No. They could be more dangerous.'

'How? In the forest there are vampires and other beasts. Then the marsh where the shadow reapers are rumoured to live. I vote mountains,' Gilbert added.

Mithos shot them an icy glare. 'One of our teams died in those mountains; fourth year warlocks then the fifth years. I don't want to risk leading third years to such a risky place.'

The Manta Academy was the only type of structure in the entire region north of the Brak'stell Bridge, so the supplies they brought would have to be rationed till they reached Brak'stell. Apart from the mountains behind the academy, Manta was a land of lush green meadow surrounded by mountains broken only by the small forest.

As the day came to a close Mithos took them to the ruins where he fought the bandits. It provided enough shelter for the night. Mithos needed rest since his mana was still low from the training session with the headmaster so the first watch was taken by the two girls.

The building in which they chose to make camp had one opening so standing watch was easy. It was the first time they had been away from the academy. Mithos had been this far before and studied maps, but he had never gone beyond the mountain walls of manta. Sara and Andria jumped when they heard a rustling coming from where the men were sleeping they turned seeing Gilbert.

'I'm relieving you, Sara,' he said in a voice only half broken. Sara always found it funny, Gilbert was powerful but his magic only worked half the time often leading him to embarrassing situations. Sara was tired and she saw Andria was just as tired having had no sleep the night before thinking about Mithos living with Sireen. They both stayed up all night calling her every name in the book. Andria complained about what that slut would do to get Mithos back whether it was true or not, Sara didn't know. Sara woke Mathew to take his turn at standing watch so Andria could get some sleep. As Sara laid her head down she heard Andria creep in the room sitting down next to her.

'You OK, Andria?' Sara asked only half awake.

'Yeah, I'm OK, just tired,' Andria replied in a whisper before wrapping herself in a blanket.

Sara awoke to find Mathew and Gilbert fast asleep. Looking to the door she saw Mithos. He was poking the embers of the small fire he had set up in the night. He had a pan on the fire, the smell of cooking bacon and sausages filled the crumbling building.

Mathew was woken by Sara, but Gilbert woke as a plate of bacon was waved under his nose. Sara and Andria sniggered as Gilbert took the plate, stuffing a slice of bacon in his mouth. They all finished their food fast as they were eager to get on their way, Mithos more than the others since last night he couldn't shake the feeling that he was being watched.

Death entered Lucian's throne room in the tower of fate. Standing in the middle of the circular room, Death took a knee and bowed his head.

'My lord, the item you requested I have it.'

Death held out what looked like the base of a pyramid; it was silver with a small hole on each side. In front of him a pedestal rose from the floor, it was like a part of the floor, the surface had a shallow square hole in it.

'Place it in the pedestal,' Lucian said.

Death did as he was ordered. Once in place the pyramid changed from silver to gold.

'My lord, how did you do that?' Death asked.

'I have found that this room takes on the shape its master desires the towers are only part of the puzzle. The pyramid will need five gems and the top. When they are brought together here I will have the power I desire.'

Lucian smiled, his plan was coming to gather and soon he would prove his new powers, the ones he acquired by activating the tower to Horatio Strange. Lucian was receiving reports every day on how much of his army was ready, every black mage and necromancer was sworn to him along with the army of Satera, their ruler was easy to convince with the simple promise of power. How greedy these mortals become when confronted with a whiff of power.

'Everything will be ready in a couple of days,' Lucian said to himself.

Mithos and his friends had been walking for hours and were close to the Brak'stell Bridge. They could see the town on the other side. With Gilbert's appetite they didn't just need horses they needed food. Sara banned Gilbert from carrying any food since he was snacking as they travelled. The bridge was small but the town wasn't. It started on one side of the bridge and ended on the far side a couple of miles away. Mithos stopped and turned to face them.

'Sara, Andria, I want you to get us some supplies.'

Mithos gave them a small purse with fifty gold Sovrins. Mithos pointed at the tavern behind them.

'We will meet back here. Gilbert and Mathew come with me so we can get the horses. Meet here in one hour.'

As Mithos Gilbert and Mathew walked through the streets people moved aside at the site of Mithos's uniform, but people never stopped talking they heard rumours of Lucian, his army, there were even rumours of Satera joining with the army of evil Mages. It took a half hour to reach the stables on the other side of the city. The stables were small with few horses but enough for what they needed. Mithos saw a man tending the horses. He seemed to back away upon seeing Mithos, startled by the black uniform, but he quickly calmed down and greeted them with a bow of his head.

'Can I help you, gentlemen?' the young boy asked with an innocent smile.

'Yes, we need horses, five of them.'

The boy stared at Mithos.

'That will be one hundred gold Sovrans,' a man said from the doorway he was leaning on. He had a walking stick and was missing his right leg just above the knee. One of his eyes was completely white. The scars on his face told the tales of the battles he had been in.

'One hundred with full tack?' Mithos asked, the man nodded giving Mithos a small smile. He returned the kind smile as he walked up to the man. They clasped arms, the deal was done. Mithos told them he would return with his friends. Mithos, Mathew and Gilbert met Sara at the tavern. She told them that Andria was getting the last of the supplies so they decided to get a drink inside whilst they waited for Andria it wasn't a dark tavern filled with drunks it was cosy and the people seemed kind and polite. As they drank their wine they heard a commotion coming from outside they didn't pay it much attention till they heard a scream. Mithos and Mathew ran outside telling Gilbert and Sara to stay at the table. Mithos and Mathew pushed passed the people. Mithos collapsed to his knees what he saw made him sick to his stomach and angry beyond belief. Andria had been ripped to pieces, her head was put on a pole her arms and legs were wrapped like a present, her torso was on a pole next to her head, chunks of flesh had been bitten from her body parts, but her heart had been ripped out.

Mithos looked around, 'Who did this!' he yelled glaring at the people, but the more he glared at them the smaller they became. He turned to Mathew. 'Take her body down and burn it,' before Mathew could touch the body it caught fire and in a second it was all gone, that is … all but a message scorched on the floor.

'I am Fear. Pray to Lord Lucian for your lives,' Mithos read out loud, his voice powered by his anger.

'Fear, what sort of name is that?' Mathew asked.

'Lucian once told me about five towers called the towers of fate. One of them is named the Tower of Fear, he told me that they required some people called the Four Plagues of man – Fear, Pain, Death and War.'

Mathew could see tears falling down Mithos's cheeks. They saw Sara and Gilbert when they turned to face the people. Mithos saw tears in Sara's eyes.

'Andria was killed, wasn't she? That body was hers, right?' Sara asked. Mithos only nodded saying nothing.

Mithos beckoned them to follow him. They had the provisions, he took them to the stables. Mathew told the stable master they would only need four horses, but he could keep the full payment when he tried to give back twenty-five gold coins. On the horses it would take them two days to reach the forest, the horses almost halved the time it would take without them, but the main thing on Mithos's mind was the outright terror on Andria's face as if someone had held up a shroud of everything she was scared of before they butchered her.

Mithos told them they would make camp when they reached the crossroads. He was concerned the forest was small, it would only take them just over an hour to get through it, but it was dangerous. The part that worried him the most was the Fog Marsh. Unless they used the path they wouldn't come out, but to get there they would have to take the mountain pass. Without a combat mage squad that could turn out more dangerous. Riding behind his three friends Mithos still couldn't keep the sight of Andria's corpse from his mind. When they reached the fork in the road they opened their bedrolls. Gilbert and Sara gathered wood for a fire so Mathew and Mithos could be alone to talk. As Mithos sat with his back to a tree Mathew stood in front of him, the leather of his boots creaked as he swayed.

'What were we told when we were selected as combat mage candidates?' Mathew asked; there was no mistaking the irritation in his voice. Mithos knew that Mathew loved Andria, too, but when she chose him Mathew stepped aside.

'We were told don't mourn the dead till the fight is over.'

'Right, and don't you think she would want us to complete our mission?'

There was nothing else for Mithos to say, he couldn't deny his responsibility to his mission and the fact that if their places were swapped he would want her to complete hers. As Gilbert and Sara started the fire Mathew started to ration their supplies for the two-day trip through the forest.

Mithos had finally come round and started training with sealing spells and shields using the shadow seal. Chains of black mana came from the palms of his hands wrapping around the rock and with one small pull the rock was split sending small shards right at him. As the shards of stone approached Mithos held out his left hand the shield turned the stones to sand. Mathew saw Mithos training and decided to send an ice wave at him. Mithos sensed the attack and blocked it with a shield. Somehow his shield control had improved he knew he could block the headmaster's spells now and couldn't wait to complete the mission and show him the improvement. Mithos returned with a fireball sending it at Mathew who countered with a small shield curving the attack back at Mithos.

Sara and Gilbert stood at a safe distance watching the two men throwing and blocking spells. Watching the two of them Sara couldn't help but think they just wanted to make a lot of noise. She saw Mathew gather violet mana in his hand it was a spell used to cripple an opponent surging through the nerves severing the brains control over the arms and legs. Mathew threw it, but the attack was dispelled by Mithos's shield. After Mathew's spell had been dispelled, Sara grabbed the cooking pot and banged it with the wooden spoon before they could get started again. They turned to face Sara.

'Dinner's ready guys so stop playing and eat.'

With their training and the image of what happened in the town burning in their minds they had forgotten how hungry they were till Sara mentioned the word dinner. They all grabbed a bowl for the soup the rich aroma filled the air. Mithos enjoyed the soup, the piping hot liquid it was very filling. After they finished eating Mathew and Gilbert washed the pot and bowls as Mithos and Sara packed the supplies. It would take at least another day to reach the marsh.

'When we reach the forest we will be on foot the rest of the way.'

When Gilbert and Mathew arrived the horses were saddled up and ready for the last length to the regal forest.

Mithos, Sara, Mathew, and Gilbert arrived at Regal Forest. Before they could enter, however, they had to retrieve all the supplies they could carry without weakening their battle strength. Mithos gave them all their ration packs making sure Mathew kept his eye on Gilbert to make sure he didn't eat all of his rations. 'It will take us two days to reach the Diagon River, but we must be careful, the vampires won't be defeated easily and they hunt in force and they may have sworn allegiance to Lucian.'

As the sun set, Mithos found it strange that they weren't attacked. He had heard stories about the vampire attacks, he was sure they always struck by the first sunset.

Chapter Six

Orden awoke, as he did every morning, to his servant Nathan's smiling face.

'Good morning, sir, you have a busy day ahead of you.'

Orden struggled to blink away the sleep from his eyes.

'Good morning, Nathan,' Orden replied as he shed the blanket and looked across the room. Nathan had set up five tabards, all silk, each with a black leather belt, black boots and leather armbands. Each armband held the crest of the Cameron clan, crossed swords with three arrows facing up. He chose to wear the green tabard. On the left side of the chest was the family crest embroidered in gold.

'What is scheduled for today?' Orden asked as he started to dress.

'First you have breakfast with your family, then you have sword practice with Legit Marcosious, after that you have military strategy studies with your father and then the rest of the day is yours, sir.'

As Orden finished lacing up his boots he noticed a small box on one of his bookshelves. He picked up the box and turned to face Nathan.

'What is this?'

Nathan bowed his head, 'My lord, it is a gift from me happy birthday, sir.'

Orden opened the box to reveal a gold ring it was in the shape of a sword. He removed the ring from its box. It was the length of his middle metacarpal. Where the blade met the cross guard was a small perfect emerald.

'It is beautiful, but how could you afford it?'

'It is a family heirloom I inherited it when I turned sixteen. I was going to give it to my son when he turned sixteen, but since he died with my wife and I'm getting too old and I have known you since you were born I would like you to have it.'

Orden looked at the ring on his hand it was beautiful. 'Thank you, Nathan.'

Fully dressed, Orden made his way downstairs. He saw his mother, father and younger brother waiting at the dinner table.

'Orden, you are late,' Mr Cameron yelled.

'I'm sorry, Father, I overslept.' Orden stood facing his father. Mr Cameron started to smile as he approached his eldest son pulling him into a hug.

'Happy birthday, son,' Mr Cameron whispered Orden pulled away from his father. 'Come and sit, breakfast is nearly ready.' Orden took his seat on his father's right side, his younger brother on the left and their mother opposite his father. Mr Cameron was staring at the ring on Orden's right hand.

'That is a fine ring, where did you get it?'

'It was a gift from Nathan.'

Before his father could ask the next question the first course was brought to the table, a wide selection of summer fruits green grapes red apples oranges and watermelon. A cup of tea was placed in front of each plate. They all bowed their heads before they began to eat.

'We offer this prayer to the divines who guide and bless us, we thank the God of War for our success as a military family.' They raised their heads to look at Mr Cameron to be the first to start eating. Sateran tradition is for no one to talk whilst eating a course. Orden took an apple and a bunch of grapes as he slowly ate. Orden saw his parents weren't too hungry. After the first course was finished they were allowed to talk till the meat course was served.

'Orden I have spoken to your swords' instructor and we have agreed that you are ready to enter the army as an officer candidate.'

Orden was shocked; he was always told he couldn't enter the army till he was eighteen. 'But I thought I had to be eighteen to join.'

'No that is just the age when my father thought I was ready, but you seem to have more of a talent than I do.' After the second course of meats and bread was consumed, Orden couldn't keep his mind off what his father had said – he was finally going to enter the army.

'Father, if I am going to the army tomorrow then can I have today off to see my friends?' Orden's mother and father stared at each other for a while with a smile from his mother. Mr Cameron turned back to face his son.

'Of course you can, but after you have come with me to the registry office. We can go now if you like.' Mr Cameron said.

'Yes please, Father,' Orden replied.

After they finished their tea Orden and his father headed out in to the city. Minos Street was quiet as normal, so the walk to Merchant Road was quite pleasant. As they came to the first street off Merchant Road, Orden saw it for the first time, the army registry office. Inside the office, Orden saw the battle scenes carved into the white marble walls, there was a single desk, and behind the desk was the recruitment officer; on spotting them he rose from his seat.

'General, sir,' the officer said thumping his fist to his chest in solute.

'At ease, Captain, I am here to enlist my son as an officer cadet.' Mr Cameron took out two pieces of parchment. 'These are recommendations from senior ranked officers who helped train him.'

Orden's father handed over the parchment, the officer looked them over. As Orden and his father took a seat the officer took out a piece of blank parchment from his desk.

'OK please give me your full name and age,' the officer said.

'Orden Cameron, age sixteen.'

'OK. Distinguishing features blond hair, blue eyes and a scar over the right eye, fair complexion so you are pure Sateran is this correct?'

'Yes, sir it is.'

The officer handed the parchment to Orden. 'OK, your hair needs to be in a braid whilst in uniform, and as of right now you are an officer cadet in the Sateran army.' He took out a black purse from the desk and slid it over to Orden. 'Half a day's pay ten gold Sovrins and twenty silver marks. You leave tomorrow. If you don't have a uniform then I can take you to the quartermaster,' the officer said.

'No need, he has a uniform, let's go Orden.'

Orden returned home with his father, his mother braided his hair whilst his father retrieved the uniform. As it was brought out Orden felt proud that he would finally be wearing the uniform of his country, he was to wear the blue tabard and cloak of the officer cadet, but the black leather armour signified he was an officer no matter the rank. When his mother finished braiding his hair she tied it off with a blue ribbon and Orden could finally wear the uniform. With Nathan's help the belt was fastened and the gladiolus sword was buckled to the belt on his right side. He held his helmet under his left arm gripping the hilt of his sword. Orden turned to face his parents.

'Every inch the Sateran soldier, my boy,' Mr Cameron said. 'Why don't you go for a walk and see your friends now, son?' Orden's mother added.

'Yes, Mother, and thank you, Father.'

Orden walked down Tavern way where he saw his friends. He found it wearying to wear the cloak, and the sword felt heavy on his hip, but he would get used to that. He stopped outside the Hammer and Sickle Inn where his friends always hung out. Entering the tavern Orden was spotted by Duncan, the blacksmith's apprentice and Orden's best friend.

'Orden, I barely recognized you. I take it you joined the army today?' Duncan asked.

'Yes I did, so any gossip today?'

'Yes, you know Lord Solis? Well he was killed last night. They say from the way he was killed it was the crimson order. You know, the assassins guild. Apparently, they saw a young woman dressed in black leather leaving his home.'

Orden took the seat next to Duncan. 'Where are Sara and Varric?' Orden asked.

'They should be here soon.'

Whilst they waited for their friends Orden and Duncan each ordered a cup of wine. Orden and Duncan had just started their second cup of wine when Varric and Sara walked in unlike Duncan and Orden who showed their pure Sateran blood with blue eyes and straight golden blond hair, Varric was only a quarter Sateran with wavy red hair and brown eyes. Sara was half Sateran, her hair was a wavy brown with blonde highlights and hazel eyes. Normally Sara was well groomed, but it looked like she and Varric had been running round the city.

'Orden, bad news,' said Varric between deep breaths.

'Nero is heading to your home with a few of his thugs,' Sara added.

Orden grabbed his helmet and in a dead run left his friends. Nero was a noble like Orden, but he was well known for extorting money from people, using his middle class thugs to beat or even kill members of their families. As he entered Minos Street, Orden saw he was followed by soldiers. He stopped when he saw Nero and his little gang.

'Stop, Nero,' Orden yelled as he prepared to draw his sword. Nero turned to see who called him.

'Ah, Orden, my old friend, how are you today, if you want to catch up you will have to wait, I'm in the middle of business.'

Orden looked up to double check the house Nero was about to threaten, it was his home.

'You know that this my home.'

Nero looked from Orden to the house then back to Orden in mock surprise.

'Really well then you owe me quite a lot of back privilege tax.'

It was the same shake down Orden had heard about the past month.

'For what exactly?' Nero put on the sadistic smile Orden hated so much.

'For the privilege of being left alone, and for my men not getting your family's blood on their blades.'

Orden gripped the hilt of his sword. Looking to his left and right, Orden saw six soldiers all wearing the brown of common soldiers, they held their shields in their left hands and were ready to draw their swords at the first sign of trouble.

'I am no merchant you can bully around, you and your thugs dare come to a noble house whose patriarch is a general in the imperial army, you are all brave if not stupid.'

Nero's left eye started to twitch, a sign of his short temper.

'As I remember I was the one who gave you that scar over your right eye, should I give you another on the left side?'

'Try it and I will finally have my excuse to forever silence that filthy mind of yours.'

Nero drew a dagger as he brought and as he attacked with it Orden brought the hilt of his sword to Nero's nose breaking it in a splash of blood. As Nero fell the soldiers drew steel taking up formations to protect their officer. Without an order from Nero the middle-class thugs started to attack, they were struck down by shields and swords splitting open the muscles of their legs Orden made it through the soldiers defence with enough time to wound a couple but the thugs were soundly defeated in mere minutes.

As the soldiers separated Nero from his gang of cutthroats he began to stand holding his nose in an attempt to stop the bleeding. 'You will pay for this, Orden Cameron, mark my words.'

Nero and his men ran off in every direction in order to stay clear of the soldiers. Orden's father burst out of the house disturbed by the commotion.

'Orden what happened?'

'Nero was about to extort us, Father, then when I stopped him he attacked me, these soldiers came to my aid.'

Orden's father looked over the six men, 'Thank you, men I shall reward you all.'

The sergeant thumped his fist to his heart in salute.

'Sir, we ask nothing in return we were honoured to help your son in battle.' The soldiers left in hast to return to their posts. As Orden locked the door of the house his mother rushed to him seeing the blood on his hands.

'Oh dear, what happened?'

'Nero, he attacked me with his thugs but they have been seen off.'

Mr Cameron brought a cup of red wine handing it to Orden. The family tradition after a battle was for the victor to drink red wine, even for a small scuffle.

'Mother, Father, I will leave for Veran training camp tonight. Nero will leave you all alone, it is me he wants.'

As Orden finished packing his father entered the house. His mother, younger, brother and Nathan were standing near the door waiting to say their goodbyes. Orden stopped just short of his family.

'Nathan, it has been a pleasure knowing you, Mother I will miss you.' Orden hugged his mother and clasped arms with his brother, turning his back on his mother and brother coming face to face with his father.

'Good luck, Orden, I shall miss you.'

'And I you, Father, you were gone for a while, though.'

His father held out a sword the handle was ebony the guard solid gold with a golden serpent wrapped around the scabbard. Orden drew the blade it was well cared for.

'It is for you, I know you prefer two swords.'

Orden hooked it to his belt; it did look good on his left hip. Mr Cameron opened the door.

'What are these men doing here father?'

'They are recruits, just like you, and they are on their way to Veran, so I thought you could all travel together, and as the superior officer you will lead them.'

As one the platoon stood to attention, he knew his father would have quickly drilled them, but time wasn't on his side. Orden stood at the head of the platoon.

'We have a full night's march ahead of us, so let's make haste; forward march!'

Orden glanced one last time to his childhood home, but that was behind him, it was finally time to grow up. As Orden reached the stables on the outside of town, he spotted the stable master holding the reins to Orden's black stallion.

'My Lord, your father told me to ready your horse, good luck in your training, My Lord.'

Orden mounted the horse nodding his thanks. Orden led the platoon, marching in a column of three ranks. Outside the city the Orden saw the Plains of Ahonak – the goddess of war – it was finally happening, he was leaving his home behind and he was on his way to his new home and family.

The Plains of Ahonak was a vast expanse of wasteland. Hundreds of thousands of soldiers had died there protecting the emperor and it was the only thing between them and Veran. Orden and the other recruits kept walking till the capital was well out of sight. Orden never forgot the stories his father told him.

'The Plains of Ahonak are not to be travelled between the hours of midnight and three in the morning.'

Orden looked to the recruits they were shivering in the cold, they had to make camp. Orden held up his fist to hold the men.

'Hold! OK, fall out and get a fire going, we set of at first light.' As Orden moved to dismount one of the recruits took the reins holding the horse stable making it easy to dismount, 'Thank you for the help, what's your name?'

The recruit stood to attention, 'Epps, sir.'

'Your full name if you please,' Orden commanded the recruit.

'Luscious Epps, sir.'

Orden clapped the man's shoulder, 'Get some food and rest; remember we march at first light.'

The soldier thumped his fist to his heart. 'Yes, sir. Thank you, sir.'

Orden crafted a hitching post for his horse; looking out at the men he saw camp fires being, lit and pots and pans being drawn along with the few rations the men brought with them; they had only brought vegetables and hard biscuits. Looking around, Orden saw many holes in the ground every now and then he caught sight of a rabbit. It would be a cold night and the men would need meat. With that in mind, Orden grabbed his bow and quiver of arrows ready to start hunting. As each rabbit emerged Orden loosed an arrow. After an hour Orden had used twenty-six arrows, one rabbit per two men. Orden went to each and every fire and dropped the rabbits with instructions to butcher and cook them in the stew at least the men would be strong for the early morning's march.

Luscious approached Orden's small fire, 'Sir the lads and me thought you might like some stew like us you need your strength.'

Orden took the offered bowl with no word of rejection. 'Thank you, Luscious,' Orden blew on the hot stew, it was the best stew he had ever eaten. After the meat and vegetables had been eaten, Orden used the bread he had brought with him to sop up the gravy. Every meal he had with his family the food was expensive, but he was never allowed to eat stew, it was seen as peasant food. After the recruits had finished their food they went straight to sleep so they could get a fresh start in the morning Orden spent the night watching over the men as they slept. The recruits had already broken camp when Orden awoke from his nap. Luscious took over the watch for two hours with the excuse a tired officer is worse than a tired army as they would be without a leader should they come under attack. Orden's horse was brought round as he buckled his sword belt after he mounted his horse the men got into formation and waited for Orden to lead them.

'It will take three hours before we reach the training camp, move out.' The plains had no hills no trees and no grass, only the expanse of dust and sand, there was no colour to the landscape only the grey dust. The temperature in the plains had a habit of changing from blistering heat to bitter cold. The men suffered in the constant change, it happened so fast their bodies couldn't adjust fast enough. Orden dismounted and walked his horse.

'Sir, why are you walking when you could ride?' one of the men asked.

'My leg was falling asleep I need to walk it off.'

After the first hour, one of the men passed out from the severe cold.

'Sir.' Orden turned to see the soldier laying on the ground. Stopping the column, Orden walked his horse over to the man and pulled out his spear cloak, wrapping it around the soldier.

'Put him on the horse,' Orden commanded. Luscious helped put the fallen man on the horse. Orden taking the reins led the horse and the men for the rest of the trip. By the time the sun was at its zenith they could see the walls of Veran and soon after they reached the main gate.

Chapter Seven

The walls weren't as large as the capital city's, but they were still magnificent. As they approached, the gates opened, Orden saw five officers, each wore the green cloak of the dragon corp. Orden stopped in front of them thumping his fist to his chest in solute.

'Sirs, officer cadet Orden Cameron. We are the recruits from Rolstes.'

One of the officers with a steel chest plate stepped forward.

'Why is that man on your horse cadet?' the officer asked.

'He passed out from the change in temperature, sir. I thought it best to not leave him behind,' Orden replied.

The fallen soldier was taken from the horse to the hospital. The horse was stabled, but Orden and his men didn't move neither did the officers. The one with the steel chest plate looked over them.

'You are all soldiers in training. You will be here for six weeks, in that time you will learn battle formations, the chain of command and discipline, Orden Cameron is your commanding officer he has already been trained and so he will train you. In doing so he creates a bond with you. Orden you will spend the rest of the day drilling them in formations. I will send a captain when it is time for dinner.'

Orden decided to start them off with some simple marching drill watching them he saw their problem was keeping their feet in time with the man in front, but they all seemed to stop at the same time and on the same foot. But it was clear he had a lot of work to do.

When the captain came for them he led Orden and the ninth dragon corps platoon to the dining hall when the recruits got in line for their evening meal Orden noticed the foul stench of what was being cooked, food he would never feed to a pig let alone an army.

The captain pulled Orden away from the line.

'Come with me unless you want to eat that filth.' The captain led Orden through the mess hall, it was plain like any stone inn, to a double door guarded by two swordsmen, they were simple oak, but sturdy nonetheless. As they opened the odour of the bad food was washed away by the smell of proper food, the same smells that came from his kitchen at home. The walls were decorated with paintings of soldiers running in to battle, or engaged in battle. All the officers were sitting at tables. Every place had a wine chalice engraved with the symbol of the regiment they belonged to. Looking around, Orden saw the names of the officers at each place. The captain took Orden to his place at one of the long tables. As each course was served the other officers were talking about the mages and the possibility of the king siding with Lucian for the attack on the Manta Academy. After dinner the captain escorted Orden and his platoon to their barrack rooms. On their floor there were five rooms for the men, one for Orden and an office. Orden stood in front of the men as the captain spoke to them 'OK, gentlemen, today was a half day; tomorrow you will have a full day of training, starting with a fifteen mile run in full battle dress. Tonight, I want the leather on your uniforms polished and your swords cleaned ready for inspection, dismissed.'

***

Mithos heard something in the trees as they came to the end of the forest. They hadn't seen any of the vampires or any other creatures he was warned about. Mithos turned around when he heard Sara scream, someone held her by the throat. The man's dark eyes glowed blood red in the shade of the trees.

'Well, what do we have here?' the man asked with a sinister grin.

'Put her down!' Mathew yelled, the anger in his voice sliced Mithos's eardrums like a blade through water. The man sniggered seeming excited at the possibility of a struggle to come. His smile showed his fangs at that moment. Mithos knew this was a vampire.

'My name is Draven. By now you should know I'm a vampire, a very hungry one.'

Mithos remembered everything he was told about vampires they are only a threat up close, when using spells, binding spells of light are best when they hold a victim. Mithos threw the signs for light and bind. As he released his mana it twisted and turned as it struck the beast with blinding speed. The vampire let go of Sara as he screamed in pain. The spell bound the vampire to the tree. Steam came from the vampire where the light touched him.

'Why would you do this? Kill me or release me,' Draven said in gasping breaths.

'I will relieve you of the pain when you answer my questions. Where are the other vampires?' Mithos asked. He didn't blink, he kept his gaze locked on the vampire, he never thought Lucian the man who taught him everything, would have turned traitor, but at this moment it didn't matter, all that did matter was the lessons Mithos had learnt.

'They are in Lord Lucian's realm, preparing for the attack on Manta.'

'When is the attack?'

Draven gave out a scream as the light bind tightened around him. 'I don't know, we were to be told when we arrived, please let me go.'

'Is that everything you know?' Mithos asked tightening the light bind. It was so tight that the vampire couldn't talk he simply nodded trying to mouth the word please. Mithos built mana in the palm of his hand twisting it to add heat creating a fireball in the palm of his hand.

'Wait you said you would release me not kill me.'

Mithos grabbed the vampire by the throat. 'I am releasing you – it is just a more permanent release than you had in mind.'

Mithos forced the vampire's mouth open and shoved the fireball down its throat before he allowed it to expand turning the vampire to ash. Mithos dropped from the trees as the others stared at him in shock.

'What?' Mithos asked, unsure of what they seemed so surprised about.

'Why did you do that?' Mathew asked. Mithos realized they didn't receive the order. 'The headmaster has declared Lucian the enemy. A kill on sight order has been placed and as you just heard he is a part of the army which will attack our college. I will not allow anyone to threaten our family.' He looked from Mathew to Gilbert then to Sara. They still had a look of shock, but it wasn't as strong as before. 'We have to carry on, we've almost reached the bridge.'

Mithos led them out the forest the three of them stuck together keeping distance between them and Mithos maybe he should have killed the vampire in a different way. When they left the forest they saw the bridge and on the other side the fog marsh home of the legendary shadow reapers. The bridge was strong since the warlocks used this trail frequently. From what Mithos was told the ancient warlocks made a deal with the shadow reapers allowing them access through their lands. As they entered the fog they lost sight of everything, looking back Mithos lost sight of the bridge though he could still hear the river so they hadn't gone far from the bridge.

'Everyone, grab hold of the person in front of you.' Mathew grabbed Mithos's cloak. When he tugged on the cloak he took that as signal to start moving.

'Why have you come to this place?' said a whispered voice. Mithos looked around till he realized he couldn't see anything a few moments later the voice came again.

'Speak why are you here mortals?'

Mithos stopped the suddenness forced Mathew to walk in to him.

'Who's there?' Mithos yelled.

'We are they who live in the fog, one among you is a warlock and has permission to walk through our lands but the others do not.'

Mathew Sara and Gilbert got so close he could finally see them.

'Who or what is it?' Sara asked.

'They are the Shadow Reapers, don't any of you say another word let me speak to them.'

The fog around them seemed to start moving swirling faster and faster. The fog around them turned in to a white wall surrounding them; at least Mithos could see his friends clearly.

'The warlock has permission to pass through, but the others do not. Why should we let them pass?' the whispered voice said.

'I am on a mission and they are assisting me, I need you to let us pass.' Mithos, Mathew, Gilbert and Sara waited for the voice to give them an answer. Mithos was prepared for whatever came next, a dark figure started to appear in the fog.

'What is your mission?' the voice asked again.

'To gain information on Lucian Rohnal.'

The fog surrounding them burst into furious angry whispers, the voice finally came back.

'Are you enemies of Lucian?' the voice asked.

'Yes we are; he is going to start a war with us,' Mithos replied.

The voices started whispering again. It was a strange language. When it stopped the dark figure became clearer, the fog between the figure and Mithos started to vanish the figure was a man with long black hair, he wore baggy black trousers and a top tied with a white sash, he also wore a blood red sleeveless trench coat, the weapon at his hip was a black katana.

'I am Captain Neji Kujo. I will escort you through the fog; we will emerge at the bridge to Azura.' Neji turned his back to them. 'Grab my arms and don't let go.'

As they took a firm grip on Neji the fog started to gather around them again, but somehow Mithos knew they were moving.

**

Orden and the other officers gathered their platoons on the parade ground having received the message that the Legit has called a parade as he walked on stage the regiment was called to attention.

'Men and women of the Sateran army, Lord Drake Rohnal has been killed and succeeded by Lord Lucian Rohnal, long may he rain over us, furthermore he has declared war on the Manta academy the bulk of the army is gathered at the Taka river where most of you are going only the dragon corps platoons seven eight nine and ten shall remain here to act as a guard unit, Orden Cameron …'

Orden stepped forward when his name was called, 'Yes, sir.'

'You will be in command here I urge you to study the maps in my office from what I was told you have a good heat for tactics.'

'Yes, sir thank you, sir,' Orden called out, proud of his new position as temporary commander.

'The rest of you form up by the rear gate in one hour, we are off to war.'

All except the two hundred who were called out ran to their barrack rooms to gather their kit, Legit Iraqan didn't move from the stage.

'While you are all here I want your sole focus to be on combat training just in case we call for aid, dismissed.'

Orden and the other officer cadets along with their platoons stood waiting for the regiments to move out as the legit came from his office all eyes turned to him as he approached a soldier holding the reins to his horse no one said a word as he mounted his steed. Wheeling, it passed the platoons that were staying; Orden took in the sight of every man knowing that many of them would not come back. As the Legit passed by the four platoons they thumped their fists to their hearts to salute him he rode to the front of the column.

'Dragon corps, twelfth Legion, first Legion forward march,' the legit yelled before they left for battle.

Mithos opened his eyes to see a bridge made of stone either side of the bridge was a deep pit, it was so deep he couldn't see the bottom. Looking back, Mithos saw Neji standing just inside the fog.

'This is where I leave you, from here it's about five hours to Lucian's lab,' Neji said before disappearing back into the fog. Mithos stared at the bridge wondering why there were no guards posted. The vampire said he had an army but he doesn't even protect his own layer. Mithos couldn't even see any runes or other magical traps. Mithos was the first to walk across the bridge as he suspected no traps were in place, but it didn't mean there weren't traps ahead of them. Looking around Mithos saw that Azura was a barren wasteland, the few trees that still stood were burned black as coal, black as the ground they walked on; every now and then Mithos saw a skull or a full skeleton lying around. It was clear from the way the bones were broken or from the charring that they were killed by magic. Some of the markings Mithos recognized all too well, one bone was someone's leg, the cracks running down the bone was the result of a spell Lucian had taught him in secret, only recently had Mithos learnt of its forbidden nature.

After an hour Mithos could finally see a tower in the distance, though it was still a long way off the fact that Mithos could see it told him how big it was, though it was the only change to the landscape and from how it looked there would be no other change.

'Mithos what are we going to do when we reach the tower?' Mathew asked.

'We are to scout out the tower and see if he still uses it.'

'We know that, he meant what's your plan once we get there?' Sara added.

Mithos turned his gaze from his friends back to the road, 'We will wait till night before we begin, Gilbert is very skilled at detection magic using that we can learn the layout of the tower and wear the highest concentration of mana is, then we can use your skills in enchantment you can spell our clothing so we can blend in to the surroundings inside the tower.'

'But what if we are discovered?' Gilbert asked.

'Mathew and I are the most skilled in destructive magic his skill in ice and water style spells and mine in lightning and fire plus the energy spells we know, very few mages in there will be able to stand against us.'

No matter what he said to try and reassure them even Mithos didn't believe they would survive a battle in there no matter how hard they fought.

Chapter Eight

Professor Narutak ran to the headmaster's office.

'Headmaster, we have received a report of an army approaching from the west.'

The headmaster turned to face professor Narutak, 'How close are they?' the headmaster asked.

'They had passed the ruins of the old kingdom when we received the report, sir, that was an hour ago.'

The headmaster turned to his window he saw the students enjoying their break eating lunch laughing and just enjoying their youth.

'Are we sure they pose us a threat maybe they are just passing by?'

'No, sir, it was a quad scout and he was the only one to make it back alive injured but alive,' Professor Narutak said.

'Have all teachers and combat mage officers report here at once that includes the Warlock commanders, they have ten minutes.'

Less than ten minutes after Professor Narutak left the teachers and senior officers of the combat mages and the warlocks started to arrive, within the ten minutes everyone had arrived ready to receive their orders.

'We have received reports of an army approaching our walls, so we must prepare for the probability of an attack,' the headmaster announced.

'Sir, what army is it?' Captain Strange asked.

'They are marching from the west the only army that way large enough to hope to attack us is Satera,' the headmaster replied.

'But why would Lord Rohnal attack us?'

'I have received a report about five minutes ago, Lucian killed Lord Benjamin Rohnal and took over the rule of Satera,' said Doctor Carmine.

'Then we have no other choice, we must prepare for the attack, order the shield squad to the wall they must reinforce the barrier on the outer and inner walls, also send the trapping corps to the wall, have them conjure runes around the outer wall for half a mile around the perimeter.'

'Headmaster our top priority should be to move the students to the mountain pass,' said Professor Narutak.

'The senior students must stay within the second wall as the younger students are moved,' Doctor Carmine added.

'Agreed, as for the rest they will be placed in the outer wall to ward off the attack sound the alarm and pass along my orders.'

The teachers and officers quickly carried out the strategy put forth by the headmaster who watched the movements of the enemy from the security room. As the Sateran army reached the ruins outside the Academy General Curu'san halted the army. He saw three men standing in front of them all dressed in red trench coats with black flames they wore cone shaped bamboo hats that covered the top half of their faces.

'Who are you three? Stand aside or you will be killed as enemies of Satera.'

The man in the centre approached the general.

'I am Death, servant of Lord Lucian and the supreme commander of both his mages and the Sateran army.' Death handed a letter to the general it bore the seal of the lord Rohnal. As the general read the letter he realized it was true.

'Sir what's wrong?' asked Legit Cor'vac.

'From the office of lord Lucian Rohnal I hereby appoint the mage known as Death as supreme commander of all Sateran forces both human and mage alike. What are your orders, sir,' the general asked bowing his head in submission to his new commander.

'Everyone will move in formation Mages at the front soldiers at the rear. Pain, Fear and I shall take the lead.'

It didn't take them long to reach the walls of the academy, the general lent down, 'Lord Death, what shall we do?'

'The field is covered in runes and it seems the barrier has been reinforced.'

Death turned to the man on his right hand side.

'Pain, the trapping corps are on the other side of the wall, bring it down, the demolition will distract them causing the seals to dissolve and the spells to be lost.'

One of the three men stepped forward muttering to himself getting louder and louder as he approached the walls.

'No one can know pain till they are known by Pain, you will know pain you will all know pain.' Stopping just short of the wall stretching out his hands, white light moved in strikes of electricity from one finger to another until the light enveloped his hands. The one called Pain drew his hands back then thrust them forward sending a massive blast wave of white light as it hit the wall it began to crack and split till it couldn't stand the force of the attack.

The headmaster watched as the wall was ripped apart sending the debris into the trapping core crushing the ones who didn't move two of the Sateran soldiers thinking it was safe to charge as they hit the barrier they burst into flames. As the dust from the wall settled Death saw the mages behind the barrier each mage was on their knees keeping their hands clasped to focus their mana, he quickly realized they wanted the black mages to waist their manna trying to bring down the barrier.

'Fear they have linked their mana so we only need one to be distracted to bring down the barrier.'

Fear locked his gaze on one of the mages and focused his mana. Death didn't know which mage was chosen till the mark of Fear appeared on the forehead of a mage. As soon as he saw the star of fear he, Death, knew the one who had been chosen; the mage who bore the mark started looking at the people beside him, when the F appeared in the centre of the star the mage started acting up, the other mages noticed his mana wavering, but before they could stop him he broke his concentration. The mage pointed at the one to his right.

'How did you get here, Lucian what are you doing here?'

The other mage looked confused, 'What are you doing? I am not Lucian, now hurry and get back in position before they attack.'

It was no use the mage attacked his friend destroying him in a blast of orange flame. Death saw the barrier come down and realized it was his only chance to keep it down so they could begin the true assault. In a flash Death was upon them, Pain and Fear used their special abilities, now it was his turn combining his hand sign with his special mana he activated his power – the black fog of death enveloped his hands. One by one Death touched the barrio corps mages. After touching seven mages he finished the spell by fluctuating his mana, in less than ten seconds the seven mages dropped dead. Death turned back to the general opening his trench coat revealing his black Katina.

'General, it is time give the command to attack.' Death waved to the black mages ordering the attack to begin. The black mages launched a barrage of fire ball attacks. The remaining members of the barrio corps leapt to action throwing up a dome shield as the balls of fire hit the shield they lit up the dusk sky, the flashes of orange and red distracted from the sun as other academy mages started to gather ready for their counter attack, but soon after the fire balls stopped the Sateran army opened fire, the volley of arrows hit while most were stopped by the barrier. Some broke through since the fire balls weakened it, every arrow that broke through hit their mark wounding and killing the mages they hit. The Sateran soldiers started their charge at the section of wall that had been destroyed by Pain. The archers and black mages kept up their attacks giving the infantry time to reach the enemy. The headmaster watched as his students were being cut down.

'Master we need to act. Let us attend the battle field,' asked one of the warlocks.

The headmaster watched as the Sateran infantry poured inside the walls of the academy swords and pikes drawn ready for the kill, the combat mages met them head on swords drawn. Their training allows them to infuse their mana with their weapons allowing a stronger swing that could cut their victims in two. The headmaster and warlocks watched as the battle raged on, they watched their friends get killed as the Sateran army washed over them like a wave of steel and green uniforms. It wasn't long before the black mages joined in the battle.

'Headmaster we must help them or it will be too late.'

The headmaster didn't answer he just watched the battle. The three in read trench coats embroidered with black flames stayed out of the battle, but it didn't stop the warlocks from feeling concerned.

'Master,' the warlocks yelled, fed up with waiting.

'Be quiet. Whether you know it or not I have a battle plan. If you hadn't, noticed most of our mages are behind the inner wall, we however shall wait for Lucian and the rest of his army,' the headmaster replied.

'The rest of his army, what do you mean, sir?' Siren asked.

'Lucian won over the vampires and other beasts not to mention that this is only a fraction of the Sateran army.'

Death, Fear and Pain watched as the army of humans and mages stormed the academy.

'Death, why haven't the Warlocks shown themselves yet?' Fear asked.

'It would be better to ask why most of the Mages are hiding behind the inner wall, but to answer your question they are waiting for Lord Lucian or us to enter the battle, now that I think about it, that isn't a bad idea.' Death looked from Fear to Pain and smiled. 'Pain go and enter the battle, it is time to call their hand.'

Pain smiled as he started walking towards the battlefield. As the Sateran army pushed the Mages back to the teachers' building, the ground beneath them started to explode. The black Mages looked at their feet, too late they realized they had walked into a mine field of exploding runes as each of the key runes exploded they set off a chain reaction causing explosions all over the front garden causing the Sateran soldiers to retreat along with most of the black mages; though they were escaping the runes they were still being bombarded by fire and lightning spells. Pain casually walked through the sea of retreating soldiers. As he made it passed the throng of soldiers and black mages he came face to face with a fireball, concentrating his mana into his hands, Pain was able to push it aside. As Pain approached the fresh mine field of exploding runes he wove three hand signs then continued walking. As he stepped on a key rune it started to explode, but instead of exploding up, the force went down making craters in the ground. As Pain reached the teachers' building he held out his hands as if holding a ball.

'Those who don't understand true pain in life shall know it in death.' A purple sphere with a black core appeared in his hands, thrusting his hands forward Pain launched the ball. As it spread out over the building hundreds of blood curdling screams filled the sky as the building and the people inside it turned to dust. Soon after, multiple explosions took place as the rest of the runes were detonated. As the dust settled what was once a beautiful garden was nothing but dirt mixed with blood and marble dust where the teachers' building once stood. Some of the warlocks cottages were partly destroyed, too, with the numerous explosions going off at the same time. Pain turned to the Sateran soldiers and black mages.

'The bulk of their force still awaits us behind that inner wall, Lord Lucian's wish is for all academy mages to die, so bring Death to them,' Pain yelled, his deep voice echoing across the battlefield. The general was the first to charge the field, followed by the black mages then the army.

Mithos, Sara, Mathew and Gilbert finally reached Lucian's lab. It was already dark and they couldn't wait anymore. Every second they waste brings Lucian closer to starting his war. Mithos and Gilbert got as close to the outside wall as they could so they could get a clear picture of how many mages Lucian had and their location in the complex.

'How many do you see, Gilbert?' Mithos asked. Gilbert dropped his concentration, 'I searched the entire compound, but there is only one life form in the entire lab and it's right inside the front door, from the aura I would say it's Lucian.'

Before they could make another move the door burst into splinters the shock wave caused Mithos and Gilbert to fall over if they had been in front of the door they would have been severely injured.

'Mithos, my boy I know you're there, why don't you and your friends come on in for a chat?'

Mithos couldn't forget that voice, the voice of his master, the man who taught him everything. Mithos walked to the opening where the door used to be, he saw the same cold eyes he remembered and had no doubt it was Lucian, even illusion spells couldn't mimic those eyes.

'What a surprise to find you here, four of my top students; tell me Mithos how are you developing?'

'My powers are growing just fine, we have come to stop you, Lucian, you have killed far too many people and you've disgraced the academy.'

Gilbert, Mathew and Sara moved into positions around the hall surrounding Lucian, he looked at each of them in turn, finally fixing his gaze on Mithos.

'You are still too weak to challenge me, even all four of you don't stand a chance. Mithos, my boy, and the rest of you, why not join me, I could make you great; for those with talent and skill like us the world is just a play thing, we should rule it as gods not cower behind self-imposed rules.'

'How far into madness have you fallen, Lucian? We can all die, we are not gods we are still human, just with different skills, how can you think you are a god when you bleed as well as any other man?' Mithos yelled what happened to make him so corrupt in morality that he would consider the world his toy? Lucian let out a large sigh.

'I guess you are still not ready, you have no idea of the powers that sleep inside you, so I'll give you a little push. You are too late to stop the war it started over two hours ago the outer walls to the academy have been breached and the combat mages are being pushed back by my army of black mages and the Sateran army. Soon I will join them on the battlefield and they will be reinforced by the vampires and my divine power.'

Mithos gripped his sword, 'You can't be allowed to proceed, it's pure madness.'

Lucian started to laugh when he saw Mithos grip his sword, 'Madness is it, am I mad to want more power, am I mad to want to be the best? No, I am ambitious.'

Lucian turned from them and started walking to the far window. Mithos had a look round the room, the stone walls were covered in scorch marks all around were alchemy components some of them Mithos didn't recognize.

'Tell me, Mithos, do you remember the stories I told you about the old kingdom, about the powers they possessed?'

'Yes I do, but they were just stories.'

Lucian chuckled, finding amusement in what Mithos said. 'I found proof in their power, we are both proof of their power.'

Mithos didn't know what to make of these deranged rantings, all he could be sure of if he wasn't sure already, was that Lucian was mad. 'You are mad, Lucian.' Mithos drew his sword, 'Your insanity knows no bounds, it's time to die, LUCIAN!'

Mithos let out a scream of rage as he charged, the intent to kill was all that consumed his mind, the man who betrayed him, the man who was destroying his home. Mithos brought his sword to a downward swing fusing his mana into the blade adding power to the swing. Lucian dodged the first attack, but without thinking Mithos attacked again each extended slash cut the walls of the lab.

'Haven't you noticed anything about the way I just moved boy?'

Mithos tried to focus and remember what happened, his strikes and his aim were dead on so how did Lucian dodge them? One moment he was there and the next he wasn't. Mithos attacked again keeping a cool head; as the mana enhanced swing reached Lucian Mithos heard the air rip as Lucian seemed to vanish. When Mithos turned around he saw Lucian still smiling.

'The air ripped, what have you done?' Mithos asked.

'This is just one power I have obtained from my studies on the old kingdom; tell me do you know why these powers were lost?'

Mithos shook his head, 'No I don't.'

'After the last war there was a lot of damage to the world, the humans finally stopped trying to destroy the Mages, in exchange they would make certain magics forbidden, such as the move I just used.'

Mithos was interested in learning more about this new type of magic, but he couldn't forget what Lucian was. This time Mithos kept a close watch as he attacked

Lucian, feeling for the use of mana; each attack Mithos launched was dead on but hit nothing but air. After a while it was clear the sword wouldn't do any good. Mithos sheathed his sword preparing to use his magic.

'Mathew, Gilbert, Sara get out of here this building is about to receive a lot of damage.'

As they cleared the building Mithos accessed his mana for his fire spells, his hands had a visible fire aura thrusting his hands forward he unleashed a stream of fire, the flames engulfed the alchemy instruments, but Lucian moved before he could be licked by the flame. Mithos followed Lucian throwing fire balls, coating the level in an inferno of flame powered by his rage. As the flames died down, Lucian jumped down from a hole in the ceiling.

'I'm disappointed, you were my favourite student and yet you can't reach me, so sad.'

It was clear that normal spells would be no use; he would have to use the five forbidden spells. Focusing his mana to his fingertips Mithos held out his hands again, the raw magic was so dense it became visible 'Recu'ro!' Yelling the spell's name made it easier to control, the purple magic melted part of the wall behind Lucian, but the new trick to make himself faster gave Lucian a distinct advantage. Mithos brought his elbows in tight against his ribs.

'Lucian, it is clear to me that I won't beat you with conventional spells so I should thank you for teaching me the five forbidden spells. I will use every power available to me in order to destroy you.'

Mithos flung out his hands, 'Amena!' Combining the black flame with all his mana the blast coated the building. It was over in seconds, the lab had been completely destroyed and turned to sand. Looking around Mithos saw his friends, they were alive and well but there was no sign of Lucian, Mithos looked around but he couldn't see Lucian anywhere it was finally over.

'Let me guess, you thought it was over.' Mithos looked behind him and saw Lucian sitting on a piece of wall that was left. 'Nice use of the divine flame my boy but it would seem that you are out of mana. Now I will offer you one more chance to join me. Imagine it, power so great one spell can defeat an army and your mana would have no limit. We would be gods what do you say?'

Lucian was right, Mithos was running on empty to keep fighting he would have to use his sword, 'I will never join you.' Lucian drew his sword, the silver cross guard gleamed in the moonlight.

'Then I will have to kill you.' Lucian used the speed trick ripping the air as he reappeared. Mithos moved from the swing but still received some damage; the blade cut his arm. As Mithos prepared to attack the air ripped as Lucian continued using his new power. Mithos heard the rip again coming from behind him. Turning, Mithos was able to block Lucian's strike.

'So you figured out how to find me then, very impressive, but unfortunately my time in this body is just about up.' Mithos was confused – his time in that body was just about up.

'Gilbert, do you see anything strange,' Gilbert nodded.

'Yes, he seems to have two auras.'

'What does that mean, Lucian, what have you done?' Mithos yelled.

'It's a power possessed by the lord Rohnal of Satera, the ability to take and control someone's soul, it allows me to show my image using the body of the soul I have taken, it's a shame but I can only use a small amount of power in this form.'

'Where are you, Lucian? We need to finish this.'

As Mithos stared at the body he saw the image of Lucian start to fade. Behind the illusion was the body of a woman, it seemed to be decomposing as the image faded. In seconds all that was left of the image was Lucian's face, the rest of the body was rotting, the stench of decay was filling the air.

'Before I go I should mention the sun is down and the vampires are free to play.'

After that last word Lucian's image vanished revealing the decomposed face of some innocent victim, how many more victims would he have? Realization came over Mithos like an avalanche, the war had already begun and he wasted time fighting an illusion they had to move fast witch meant getting help from the Shadow Reapers.

Chapter Nine

The academy mages fell back from the wall, the tide had quickly turned when the vampires joined the Sateran line the warlocks were becoming more and more impatient, it wouldn't be long before the mages were forced to the mountain pass escape route. Before any of the warlocks could speak the headmaster stood.

'It is time, Lucian is about to arrive, all Warlocks will now join in the battle switch to guerrilla tactics.'

The command they had been waiting for was finally given. The warlocks moved as fast as they could to the battlefield they were lucky Lucian's forces hadn't made it inside the buildings yet so they could move in front of the inner wall. Being dressed in black had its advantages they waited for the command from the warlock captain, the element of surprise would only work for one attack, so they had to make it count, though the vampires could see in the dark they were at the back of the army so there was little risk of them being spotted. Receiving the telepathic command from the captain, the warlocks launched a variety of energy attacks as they rained down on the advancing army they exploded at chest height for maximum damage the confusion didn't last for long as the vampires leapt over the soldiers ready to strike the warlocks, but they were ready for such a predictable move as the vampires landed some of the warlocks fell screaming, Captain Lawrence saw one of his men with five arrows sticking out his chest, the vampires leaping was a cover for the valley of arrows loosed by the Sateran army, the remaining warlocks put up physical wards to block the next valley of arrows then switched to the offensive throwing every spell they could. Half of them drew their swords and charged the enemy line cutting down any vampire they saw, but they were still heavily outnumbered. A huge vampire armed with a claymore tried to swing at the captain, but he was combusted by a fire wisp, a summoning creature known only by the headmaster. Looking around, the captain could see hundreds of the fire and lightning wisps. Wisps were small spirits whose colour showed the element they were connected to. As they passed through a target they would either burn, receive an electrical shock or be blown up. They were a powerful ally and a terrible enemy. It was a morale boost, seeing the headmaster pulling out some of his most powerful spells to help drive back the invaders. Looking up at the inner wall, the captain could see a small portal, swirling patterns of orange red and purple were beautiful, but it told them that Lucian had just arrived. The headmaster's blue aura grew more and more intense, the air around him seemed to explode with lightning the raw power was overwhelming.

'Lucian you have finally arrived, now I ask that you pull back your army and forget about this pointless crusade, the power you seek doesn't exist,' the headmaster pleaded, hoping that his once favourite student would listen to reason.

'Come on, old man, this is just the beginning of the war that I will lead, the army that did this is a small fraction of the one I control, not to mention the powers I have obtained from my experiments and research into the old Kingdom. What more is there for a mage if not to become powerful?'

'Lucian, since you were left here I raised you like a son hoping that you would take up my ideals and become the next headmaster, I never dreamed that you would become so corrupt with power.'

Waving hand signs they prepared for battle.

'Tell me one thing, Master, what do you know about the tower concealed by the Manta Mountain's?' Lucian asked.

'It was built by the mages of the old kingdom, they saw the mistake they had made and feared someone misusing it.'

'Then tell me why didn't they destroy it? I will tell you – because they couldn't the magic was too great for them to control so all they could do was seal it away. They called them towers of fate, but I prefer to call them divine towers.'

'You say towers like there are more than one.'

'There is the Tower of Fear, the Tower of Pain, the Tower of Death and at the centre the Tower of Hope. When they are all activated the tower of hope will endow the one who sits on the throne with the powers of a god, and I alone shall have that power.'

'Lucian, you are truly mad and it looks like I have to be the one to stop you.'

'Madness is a point of view; I think you are mad for letting this incredible power go to waste. So I will show you what I have gained.'

Lucian launched a fire ball, the headmaster warded the attack launching into his own. Lucian dodged the lightning bolt; as the dust cleared the section of the wall where Lucian stood had been destroyed. Who was this old fool to stand between him and greatness? Lucian drew his sword running his mana through the blade infusing it with fire magic. The headmaster did the same with lightning magic. The wisps that were attacking his army changed their attack direction and headed straight for Lucian. Whirling his sword around he sliced the first of them they vanished in an explosion of lightning and fire; one by one Lucian continued slashing cutting and hacking at the elemental spirits lighting up the sky with a mix of blue red and orange. As he defeated the last of the wisps Lucian saw Siren and Sireen standing next to the headmaster.

'Lucian, I give you this last chance before I kill you,' the headmaster said.

Lucian looked behind himself and saw Pain, Fear and Death.

'No, old man, since you are surrounded I give you this last chance.'

The twins drew their swords holding the blades to the back of the headmaster's neck.

'So you two have betrayed us, fine then you will all die.'

The headmaster stepped off the wall and started to fall.

'Death, Pain, Fear, Siren and Sireen take care of the warlocks, leave the old man to me, there will be no holding back from this point on,' Lucian commanded.

As his generals dropped down from the wall the headmaster rose on the back of his summoning creature the, Falcon of Storms, a powerful and ancient lightning bird. Lucian had heard the legends that the element is so closely tied with this creature that it appears to glow blue.

'It would seem the legend has been confirmed, but remember, old man, you are not the only one with access to a legendary beast.'

Lucian focused all his mana in his summoning, placing his hands on the ground he marked the appearance of the summoning rune completing the summoning, as

Lucian's creature appeared more of the inner wall was being demolished the last of the red dragons was finally going to aid him in battle.

'So, old man, what do you think? Be honest now ...' Lucian was quite pleased with the bewildered look on his master's face.

'Very impressive, I take it that is the last great red dragon, Ceara, he truly is powerful.'

Ceara moved to attack, spitting fire at the falcon who evaded the attack and countered by diving at the huge lizard with its sharp talons, just barely scratching the dragon's neck.

'Dava is that the best you can do? I expected more from you, but I can see you are getting as old as your master just ripe for plucking,' said Ceara in his roaring voice. Ceara and Dava continued their fight in the air quickly demolishing the inner wall Pain finished the job by destroying a huge segment allowing the army of mages, Sateran soldiers and vampires to push through, they walked over the bodies of the warlocks and smashed into the remaining force of combat mages. Looking at the far end of the grounds, Death saw that the bridge and path to the mountains had been destroyed. Pain, Fear, Siren and Sireen had joined him.

'Well, the escape route has been destroyed, so all the ones you see here are it, have fun and kill them all.'

The mages on both sides were too low on mana reducing most to picking up swords and battle axes, most of them were out of their element with swords since they spent their lives honing their skill with magic, Death activated his power, the black power of death covered his hands. Using his superior speed he ran from one mage to another, each mage he touched was marked for death, a sudden surge of mana to either hand sealed the spell killing the marked. Fear was making them kill their

96

friends and Pain was evaporating them. The screams of those poor mages drowned out the battle cries of the Sateran army and slightly dimmed the sound of Lucian's battle above them.

Lucian's dragon spat a thin line of fire at the headmaster, each blast just missed when the falcon dodged.

'Master you do know what happens if you or your creature dies right?' Lucian asked.

'Yes the same as yours when a soul-linked creature dies so does the one who summoned it, but I don't think I should worry about that since I have had enough with this game.'

The headmaster put his hands on the back of Dava causing the space around the falcon to become electrified if Lucian's dragon touched that area they would both be finished. As Dava dived for Ceara the dragon flapped its mighty wings rising just above the lightning barrier.

'So, Master, you are using your life force to try and defeat me, you old fool, I possess the power of the ancients, their tomes and magic course through my veins the magics they created give me abilities far beyond your comprehension and soon I will become a god and you will be dead.'

Lucian thrust his hands forward shooting a ray of azure light, it touched the tip of Dava's wing just slicing the tip of its feathers. Holding his right hand over his left and focusing his mana the blue mana turned to red and in the centre was a black flame.

'This time you won't escape my power,' Lucian yelled as he threw the red ball. Dava tilted, dodging the ball. When Lucian held out his open right hand as he clenched his fist the red ball expanded to pure black flame, it touched Dava's tail feathers setting them alight, the huge expanse of flame extinguished but the fire on Dava's tail remained.

'It's over master, this is the complete divine flame.'

In a second the fire changed to purple and engulfed half of Dava's body causing the falcon to fall from the sky the headmaster jumped when he was close enough to the wall and watched as Dava became completely consumed by the fire. The Headmaster clutched his hand to his chest Lucian jumped from Ceara before the Dragon flew away.

'You feel it right, Master, your heart is failing because Dava is already dead.'

Lucian with his sword drawn knelt next to the headmaster who had fallen to the floor, 'You will be dead by this time tomorrow, till then I leave you with this little bit of information, my sword and blood is Sateran as you know, any cut will bring pain if you are near someone with Sateran blood that is increased if they have pure blood like me and my son.'

Lucian ran the edge of his sword across the headmaster's arm allowing the Sateran magic to enter the old man's bloodstream.

'Now, before I go just nod your head yes or no, have you met Mithos's other half yet the evil within?' the headmaster nodded having run out of strength. 'Good, I can't wait to see the result of that experiment.' Grabbing the headmaster Lucian's shadow slid from the wall to where the teachers' building was where he laid the old man down. He used the same technique to reach his army before they began their final charge.

'Stop, all of you are to fall back now, no more killing today, we shall return to the Sateran border.'

'But why, my lord, we are winning?' asked one of the officers.

'Don't question, Lord Rohnal, you will follow orders or die a traitor,' Death warned.

The vampires, black mages and Sateran soldiers cleared the area, but Lucian stopped just on the other side of the outer wall.

'Well, my old friends, this is where we say good bye, and it's time to die.' Lucian held out his hand, 'Hi'zen!' he yelled as a ray of white light covered everything from the inner wall to the mountain escape the ground began to be ripped apart as the destructive wave pulsed, every building and wall segment crumbled to rubble and every mage caught in its wake was torn to pieces.

***

Mithos and his friends arrived at the entrance to the fog marsh. After three steps Mithos started to hear the voices again, whispers in the fog.

'Shadow Reapers, I need to speak with you.'

The fog began to swirl around them again Mithos knew they were surrounded by Shadow Reapers.

'Speak, Mithos,' said the whisper.

'That power that allows you to move through the fog in minutes, have you ever taught it to Lucian?'

The dark figures appeared in the fog, one stepped forward, it was Neji.

'No one has ever taught that to a mere mage, not in over three thousand years, it is forbidden.'

'Then why does Lucian have the ability to move faster than sight and not need a fog to do so?' The whispers erupted all around them in a language that Mithos didn't know.

'That technique is called the shadow slide what we use is shadow sprint.'

'Could he have learned it from some sort of tome?'

'No only five of us have mastered it and one of them vanished ten years ago, but even he wouldn't defile that law.'

Mithos turned to his friends then back to Neji.

'Lucian has that power, when he moves it sounds like the air is being ripped.'

More whispers exploded from the Fog as three other Shadow Reapers emerged from the fog.

'Then we will escort you to the academy and see for ourselves what has happened.'

Each of the Shadow Reapers took hold of Mithos and his friends.

Mithos opened his eyes to find they had arrived outside the Academy walls, but something was wrong everything had been destroyed bodies lay all over in a bloody mess, many had received cuts and arrows and were even crushed but the ones in the worst shape were taken down by magic.

Mithos drew his sword behind him the Shadow Reapers did the same. 'Everyone spread out, search for survivors,' Mithos ordered before running to the teachers' building where he thought he saw movement. All around were demolished buildings and corpses, some were Sateran soldiers. As Mithos reached the rubble that was once the teachers' building he saw it, the body, he thought moved, battered and bruised the headmaster opened his eyes, he seemed to be in pain.

'Master, what happened?' Mithos asked holding his masters head.

'Mithos, it was Lucian; he attacked with an army of vampires, mages and Satera, they killed everyone.' The Master's breathing was laboured, to make matters worse his heart beat had almost stopped.

'You are the last Warlock since Siren and Sireen have betrayed us. It is up to you destroy Lucian.'

Mithos looked away from his master, 'I can't, he is far too powerful, there is no way I can win.'

'Don't underestimate yourself, take my sword and find allies. As the new master of the warlocks many kings owe you a favour.'

Holding his sword the headmaster released his last breath. Mithos took the sword from the old man and headed to the others. Neji and the three Shadow Reapers stood with Mithos's friends with grim expressions.

'It seems to be true. Death was among the ones who attacked here and from what you described he has violated our laws. My father gave us special orders if this was to happen. We shall accompany you and aid you in your mission to destroy Lucian and his minions.'

The four Shadow Reapers bowed their heads as they went to a knee. The three who wore hoods uncovered their heads. Two of the Shadow Reapers were women, one with long black hair the other with short red hair, both had a fair complexion, the man had short brown hair with grey eyes.

'The one with red hair is Deon, the woman with black is Areha, the man is Maxos,' Neji said. Mithos looked at his friends. Mathew was holding Sara who seemed to have broken down, he couldn't blame her; their friends the people they had known their whole lives had been killed by the man they all respected most it, hurt them all.

'Neji I need to know about Death and about the ancients' forbidden magic.'

Neji took in a deep breath and sat on the ground. 'Death as I said was one of us, his power lies in the fog that shrouds his hands, anyone who touches it is as good as dead, once touched by death he increases his mana to his hands which cuts the strings of life and the victim drops dead. As for the other request you know that we are the ancient mages we created many powers that can destroy this world several times over. After the last war we tried to destroy this power but were unsuccessful, the power was too great, so we did the next best thing and sealed them all away.'

Mithos tried to remember everything Lucian had told him. 'Lucian mentioned the power for unlimited mana, he wants to become a god and thinks he found that power. Do you know what he might have meant?'

Neji looked at the other Shadow Reapers, they all nodded before he spoke. 'Yes, there was one power, but it was the only one we created with that power and it helps shed a little light on why Death was with him. He was referring to the towers of fate. There are four of them: the Tower of Pain, the Tower of Fear, the Tower of Death and the Tower of Hope. To break the seal you need to have the power to bring instant death, great pain and fear. There were three Shadow Reapers who possessed those powers, Pain, Fear and Death, but to activate them you needed to sacrifice one thousand souls for each tower, the one who activates the tower of hope will become a god, because of its power all records of them were destroyed so Death must have told Lucian about them.'

Mithos didn't know what to make of it, he only just noticed he was gripping the headmaster's sword tight, the colour was starting to drain from his hand.

'So somehow I need to raise an army to fend off his vast force whilst I try to kill him and I need to gain enough power to fight him on equal ground and whilst we are searching for this army, Lucian will be searching for and activating these towers can anyone else say impossible?' Mithos felt lost it couldn't be done then a thought came to him. 'Wait, you ancients created the magic that Lucian knows, right then can you teach me?'

'No, most of our magic is long gone. In exchange for the ability to control the fog and live in it we gave up most of our magic. Besides, the powers Lucian has predates any living Shadow Reaper,' Neji said.

Mithos stopped talking when he heard the rubble of the old library moving. They all ran over following Mithos. The rocks were shifting and falling and as the last of them fell Mithos saw the muscular form of Ren the librarian and curled in a ball was the dwarf Cundi Ren through the huge segment of roof that seemed to fall on them.

'Damn you, Lucian, just because your book was late there was no need to destroy the library, you slug!' Ren yelled. Mithos could almost see the steam coming from his nose as he breathed deep.

'Ren how did you survive?'

The huge red-headed man turned to Mithos then he had a better look around. 'What happened here?'

'Lucian destroyed the school and killed everyone,' Mathew answered; he was still holding Sara.

'I never thought he would do all this just for a late book.'

'It's not always about your damned books!' Gilbert yelled. Cundi stood up holding a saddle bag.

'What's in the bag, Cundi,' Mathew asked. Cundi always looked a little slow and students seemed to make fun of him because of it.

'Warlock sees them.'

Mithos walked over to him, 'Cundi, I am a warlock can I see them?' Cundi held the saddle bag to Mithos.

'Warlock,' he said as his voice and mind seemed to drift.

Mithos smiled and took the bag there seemed to be scrolls, five of them, reading one of them they seemed to be debts owed to the warlocks.

'Mithos, what is it?' Gilbert asked.

'Our key to an army, debts to be called in by a warlock, the high elves, the dwarves, dark elves and two countries Nachreach and Albion.'

Neji walked over to have a look at them.

'Nachreach and Albion don't have very big armies, but Albion has the best cavalry and Nachreach have the best pikes around. The high elves are great archers and the Dark elves have the best swordsmen. But without a doubt the dwarves have the best steel, their weapons combined with the training of the others will be a force to be reckoned with,' Neji said.

Mithos put the scrolls back in the saddle bag holding it in one hand and Headmaster Strange's sword in the other.

'Which of them is the closest to us?'

Ren took a thick piece of paper from his pocket and started to unfold it. When Ren was finished unfolding the paper he showed them a map.

'It looks like Nachreach to the northwest. Albion is an island just north of there. It would be best to split into two groups since the others are to the south of us.'

Ren made a good point, but Mithos couldn't lead Lucian to Nachreach, he would have to go south.

'Mathew, Sara, Cundi, Maxos and Deon, that leaves me, Gilbert, Neji, Areha and Ren. Mathew, you guys go to Albion and Nachreach. We will head south.' Mathew took the two contracts. 'Before you go those contracts are for Warlocks, I have been named grandmaster of the Manta Warlocks so in my right I name the following recruits Mathew, Sara and Gilbert.' Mithos took three pendants from his pocket. 'These are enchanted to help shield you against element magic, but remember they only help, they aren't there to completely protect you, now find a warlock with an outfit your size and wear it. The leaders of every land know that pendent and the warlock battle dress.'

After twenty minutes, all three of them returned wearing the clothing of a Warlock. Mithos knew he couldn't let the order die, but he also knew they could become more of a target with the title.

'OK now we can leave. If you need to contact me use a summoning bird, and be careful.' Mithos watched as two of his closest friends left for their mission.

'It will be safer for them you know,' Neji said resting his hand on Mithos's shoulder.

'Sara is the one I worry about, her power can grow out of control, I saw it happen once before and it nearly killed me. To get her under control, her anger can be dangerous.' Mithos let out a slow breath as he watched his friends get further and further away. 'OK let's go; our first stop will be the Elvin city of Vor'tee.'

Chapter Ten

Orden ran across the pared ground when he heard of a messenger Orden waited when he reached the front gate the messenger dismounted and saluted, 'Sir, the war against Manta is over; the victory goes to Lord Rohnal who joined the battlefield.'

Orden found himself disappointed at not being able to fight with the Lord Rohnal. 'So what is to happen now the war is over?' Orden asked.

'No, there is a bigger war to fight and you are called to battle, this was a training camp, but considering our losses in battle we need as many soldiers as possible for the next attacks from what we have been told it is a war against the mages.'

Orden thought about it, 'Then why are we moving against the other nations?'

'World conquest is part of it.'

After Orden received his new orders he called everyone to the parade ground.

'Our war against Manta is over, but we're not stopping there, we will press on and take the world. Lord Rohnal himself will be joining in with some of the battles as he did with the Manta Academy, we are to leave in one hour and the role of trainers will be taken by retired soldiers and we will join the main force.'

The soldiers saluted before they were dismissed. It took a couple of hours before the soldiers were packed and ready at the gate. Orden and his lieutenants were mounted, Orden looked behind him and with a wave of his hand the order to march was given.

***

By nightfall Mithos Gilbert Neji Ren and Areha reached a village but it looked deserted. As they walked further into town they reached the town centre, it was littered with what looked like mummies, they looked dry, without an ounce of muscle. Mithos Areha and Neji drew their swords when they heard the string of a bow tighten.

'Drop your weapons or you will all die,' said a voice. It came from one of the building tops; they didn't drop their weapons.

'What happened here?' Mithos called back.

'This is your last warning, drop the weapons or we will open fire.'

Mithos stabbed his sword in the ground, Neji and Areha followed Mithos's lead.

'What are you doing here, mages, didn't your kind caused us enough trouble when two of your people killed most of the town?'

Mithos looked around at the bodies lying on the ground. 'What did they look like?'

People stood up the roofs of the houses, there weren't many people left but they were all armed. 'They were dressed just like you, a man and a woman, they heard that we were holding a wedding celebration and volunteered to sing for the bride and groom, they were amazing their voices seemed to touch your very soul.'

Mithos couldn't believe it why would the incest twins attack a town and what spell could they have used to cause this much damage? 'Wait, did this happen when they sang for you all?' Mithos asked. The villagers nodded.

'What is it, Mithos?' Gilbert whispered.

'It's an ancient form of magic, but as far as I knew the only creatures that could use it are banshees and they have been extinct for thousands of years. Basically, their song can soften someone's heart, but at the same time the person has their life force drained away, though I never thought they could still exist.' Mithos looked at the men aiming weapons at them he could sense there were more people than he could see, but he didn't want to push these people after what they had suffered.

'The ones who came here, did they look similar to each other and did they seem to be overly fond of each other?'

'Yes, they did and they were dressed like you,' one of the villagers yelled.

'They are Siren and Sireen, former mages from the Manta Academy, they assisted Satera in destroying it and killing my friends and family, so don't you dare say they are with me. Lucian, Pain, Fear, Death, Siren and Sireen – I won't rest till they all die. We are gathering an army to fight against Satera and the dark mages, so if any of you have skill as a soldier I would welcome your aid at my side in battle.'

Some of the people hiding between the houses came out, most of them held swords and wood axes an older man approached Mithos.

'I was in the last war with Satera and I was cut by a Sateran blade, tell me what do you know about Sateran steel?' the old man asked.

'Anyone cut will feel pain if they come across anyone with Sateran blood, it is worse if they come across one who is pure Sateran.'

'Correct, I know that you are Sateran you are pure, now tell me, after hearing this do you still want to fight against Satera?'

Mithos looked at the old man's hand; he saw the scar. 'Yes, I am a mage of Manta; as long as Satera serves Lucian I will fight and kill them.' Mithos could see the man shaking in pain as he walked closer to him.

'In that case I won't be much use in battle, but I am good with tactics and have trained many of the men here ready for the next war.'

'Elder, why would you want to help their kind? He admitted to knowing the two who killed our people, my daughter was murdered by them.'

The old man turned to face the villager. 'So all are guilty for the actions of a few, in that case don't the mages and elves have the right to wipe out all humans for the hundreds of years of slavery and persecution, by your logic what happened here still isn't enough and they could start killing randomly.'

'But that wasn't us,' the villager pleaded.

'Just like I wasn't the one who did this. It was those who eliminated almost everyone I grew up with, so tell me, do I need to be punished for the sins of others even though I haven't sinned myself? And as the old man said should you be punished for the sins of your ancestors?' Mithos asked staring the man down. The villagers lowered their weapons some returning their swords to their scabbards.

'I cannot force any of you, but I ask that you all consider helping this young man, tonight we will burn the bodies for a mass funeral, it is too late for them to leave so they will stay as our guests till morning. I ask that you all consider helping them avenge our fallen friends and loved ones.' The old man turned back to Mithos, 'Young man, you and your friends will be my guests and I ask that you please attend the funeral and remember the names of those who lost their lives today.'

Mithos was still shocked by what the twins had done. The old man's house was quite impressive almost like a small manor. So much had happened in less than a month; the destruction of the academy, Lucian starting his war and taking command of Satera, and soon there would be a full-scale war since Lucian planned to enslave everyone. Mithos was brought from his thoughts by a knock at the door.

'Come in,' Mithos said. It was the man who openly challenged Mithos in the village centre.

'The funeral fire is about to begin, please follow me.'

The man led them from the house through the village to the far end. They had spent hours preparing for this funeral fire, but it would take a while based on how many corpses there were. As they reached the village cemetery there was just a huge fire pit and no graves, the villagers that remained surrounded the fire pit, the corpses were wrapped in white sheets with names painted down the front of them. Mithos and his friends were stood in the front of the villagers as the village elder read the names of those who died from a list. After a couple of hours the villagers started to sing as the elder moved closer to Mithos.

'Mage, would you do us the honour of lighting the fire now, please?'

Mithos held out his hand normally he would skip the incantation for simple spells, but this time he said it out loud, 'By my power as a Mage I beseech the spirit of fire to grant me your divine power so I might light a blaze in your name, Breg.' The fire pit was consumed by flame, the villagers seemed to be impressed, but since Breg was a fire that could be controlled he decided to spell out a word, his promise to the departed, the word remembered reached out to the night sky in red flames.

One by one the dead bodies were consumed by flame, and as night turned to early light all that remained was a pile of ash. Many of the villagers stayed long after Mithos had retired for the night they needed rest since they were leaving early in the morning and it would take time to gather an army large enough to challenge the awesome might of Satera and the black mages.

Mithos woke early and found the old man packing a huge bag. Getting a closer look, Mithos found it to be his bag.

'Excuse me, what are you doing?' Mithos asked.

'I'm packing you and your friends some food. I'm far too old to travel with you, so I'm giving you all the aid I can, young man,' the elder replied still packing.

Mithos walked outside thinking to get in some early sword practice there would be a big probability that he would run out of mana in the fights to come, so training with a sword whilst he had the chance would be best. As he opened the door the sun bathed his face in its heat. As his eyes adjusted he saw the Elder's garden, it was well kept. Mithos walked round back where he knew there was a large grass area perfect for some light training. As he reached the back of the elder's house, Mithos saw fifteen men all dressed in heavy armour, each chest plate held the insignia of the fire spirit – a sword with a flame aura – one of them, the man from yesterday who challenged Mithos in the village centre and later took him to the funeral. The man fell to a knee and the other fourteen stood to attention.

'Lord Mithos, I apologies for what I said yesterday, please forgive a grieving father.'

Mithos was more than shocked at what he was seeing. 'I forgive your words but I understand your anger,' Mithos said in a small voice, he couldn't muster much more and he didn't know how they came about the title lord. 'My Lord, the sword you carry, my father told me about it years ago, this village swore an oath to the old master of the warlocks that when the time came for war we would swear our allegiance to the one who carried it, we are pleased to offer our skills in battle,' the man said. His head was still bowed.

'So you want to be the beginning of my army is that correct, you do know that you might all die, right?'

'Yes, My Lord and we are all prepared; we also have another gift for you.' The man held out a locket it was sealed and the word remembered was carved in the silver. 'We all have one, inside are some of the ashes of the people who were murdered by the twins. We all have one, so they can be with us in battle, I command these men, Captain Edwards at your service, sir the other five members are gathering supplies, arrows, food and tents. We even have some horses for you and your friends.'

Mithos let his breath go to calm and collect his thoughts till he could finally open his eyes and smile.

'Thank you all, I accept your help and gifts, welcome to the army, stand up, Captain.'

Edwards rose and stood to attention.

'OK, when the others are up we will need to leave. We have a lot of ground to cover and I'm sure Lucian will eventually catch on to what we are doing. We need to reach Vor'tee as soon as possible, so be ready to march.'

They all saluted and marched from the garden. Mithos knew how hard it would be to get Gilbert up. He still had at least one hour to train. As Mithos swung his sword He saw another blade block his. Neji was holding it.

'Training is better when you have a partner, defend as best you can.'

Neji went to an overhead strike. Mithos blocked as quick as he could, but Neji was fast in his next move, circling his sword and tapping Mithos's side.

'If you can't move fast then you will die fast, so it might be a good idea to show you ways to use your sword and then practice for a couple of hours when we make camp.'

Neji turned to look at the soldiers loading a wagon. 'There is safety in numbers, but there is also a chance that Lucian will notice a big group like this.'

'Do you think it's a bad idea?'

'No, it's a good idea, but we need to be more careful from now on.'

Neji swung his sword again forcing Mithos to dodge each of Neji's swings were too fast and his movements were fluid, they flowed one after another allowing for no counter.

'I trained hard every day to build my skills, but even with the thousands of years I have had there is a limit to what I can do, all my training does now is to stop my skills from becoming dull. You must train every day to use a sword in battle.' Mithos blocked a swing. 'Remember, Sateran soldiers train from a young age, every man in Satera trains from the day they can pick up a sword in case war does break out, so it isn't a simple army, it's the whole country you will be fighting.'

Mithos pushed Neji back and charged in to his attack. Neji swung as Mithos got closer, but he dived under the swing bringing his sword round at his full arm's reach. Neji did the same and they both stopped less than an inch from each other's neck.

'It seems you do know a little about swordplay; just don't go getting weak on us,' Neji said as they both sheathed their swords. As they reached the front of the house the others were ready to leave. The twenty soldiers were in ranks and they did look like professional soldiers.

'OK let's go.' As the soldiers started marching the armour made one loud sound since their steps were as one, the summer heat rained down on Mithos bathing the grass plain, it would still take a couple of days to reach the Elvin city. Though the plain was clear of trees it was a hilly terrain. There was no way to see what was coming over the next hill, so despite the time restraint they walked at a slow steady march, Mithos didn't like the feeling he was getting since the plain crossed a road that was a regular gateway out of Satera. Mithos halted the small army when he heard formation marches. They were still a good distance from the next hill but there had to be a lot of soldiers up ahead to drown out the sounds of his Army.

Chapter Eleven

The twenty soldiers moved in front of Mithos and his friends forming two ranks of ten the front rank knelt down holding up their shields and the rear rank readied their bows.

'Draw arrows,' Captain Edwards ordered.

Mithos held up his hand, 'Don't draw, just stand ready.'

Captain Edwards looked at Mithos, 'Sir, if it is the enemy we must strike first.'

'Captain, you have sworn to follow me and my orders. It is daylight with no cover, so there won't be any vampires. I can't sense any magic users, we have two mages of Warlock class and two Shadow Reapers. It would take thousands of soldiers to drain our mana. From what I hear there only a couple of hundred soldiers and they might not be Sateran and we are not killing the innocent.'

Captain Edwards looked irritated by Mithos interfering, 'But, My Lord, what if they attack?' Edwards asked.

'Then I will unleash my full power on them if you lose arrows then we weaken our efforts, correct?'

Edwards looked at the ground. Mithos and Gilbert stood in front of the small force ready to let loose their power. They waited, as the noise got closer eventually Mithos saw the officer riding in front before the rest were visible. Mithos knew they had been seen as the officer wheeled the army ready to face Mithos. The Sateran officer raised the white flag of parlay and rode towards the centre of the field. Mithos mounted his horse again, leaving Gilbert to lead in his stead. Mithos met the officer between the two forces he heard a horse galloping behind him, looking back Mithos saw Neji who stopped beside Mithos.

'He has an attendant,' Neji pointed out.

'Captain Orden Cameron of the dragon corps, this is Lieutenant McDonald of the dragon corps.' Both officers bowed their heads to Mithos and Neji.

'Mage Mithos Ronal of the warlocks, this is Neji of the Shadow Reapers,' Mithos said.

'How do you have the same name as Lord Lucian Rohnal?' Orden asked.

'He trained me before he betrayed us, the students of the Manta Academy.'

Orden whispered to his lieutenant then turned back to Mithos.

'From what I see you only have twenty-four men including yourselves, we have two hundred you are severely outnumbered. I offer you this chance to surrender. If, however, you choose to fight us today you will all have an honourable death.'

Mithos looked at his men then at the Sateran army it was true that they were outnumbered, but not outmatched.

'Captain, we have two warlocks, one mage and two Shadow Reapers I was trained by Lucian Rohnal as a combat mage and by the murdered Headmaster Strange. If you choose to fight be warned that I will be forced to unleash my full power on you so will the others, then if any of you live my soldiers will finish the rest of you. I do, however, offer you the chance to join us. Lucian will be defeated in this war, so I would advise you to join us, but, as you said, if you fight us today you will be granted a good death worthy of a soldier.'

Both sides showed no sign of surrender. There was no point in trying to reason with Sateran soldiers, they are too loyal. The leaders of both sides returned to their armies. Mithos and Neji dismounted, staying in front of his army as he watched the Sateran army preparing for battle.

'There are only two hundred of them, you will see the full power of a mage,' Mithos said.

'Gilbert, could you quickly lay some runes where I marked the field?'

Gilbert smiled as he put his hands together focusing his mana. Neji look from Gilbert to Mithos.

'Is that the reason you went out there, to leave a mana mark on the field?' Mithos simply smiled looking at the field Mithos could sense the runes appearing under the grass. Turning to Neji and Areha, Mithos could see strange marks around their eyes, as each rune appeared their smile grew wider and wider. The Sateran army started walking in line formation some at the rear notched arrows. Mithos threw up a shield ready for the arrows the archers started firing. Mithos was glad he threw up a dome shield because as the arrows hit the shield they broke and splintered. The arrows kept coming as the advancing force approached the centre of the field. As the Sateran's passed the mana marker Gilbert detonated the runes, flames engulfed the Sateran force. As the arrows stopped, Mithos dropped the shield and refocused his Mana throwing a ball of fire towards the enemy exploding over the centre of the field. The screams of the soldiers covered the roar of the flames. Orden stood after being knocked back by a blast of fire as the smoke cleared Orden saw the hundred swordsmen that were led by his lieutenant lying on the ground, some were still crawling severely burnt, but the enemy was untouched. He looked back at the rest of his force; how, in a couple of minutes, could their force, who had outnumbered the enemy, be just cut in half?

'Draw swords, if we are to die today it will be as soldiers in service to Satera.' The rest of the soldiers drew their weapons. Orden took the lead with both swords drawn. As Orden reached the centre of the field he was hit with the smell of burning flesh some of the men were badly burnt but still alive and groaning, but most were dead being blown apart by magic. He finally understood why Lucian wanted them all dead, how could the rest of the army stand fighting thousands of them without running it only took two to kill one hundred men no one should have that power. As they got closer and closer the enemy showed no sign of attack.

'Surrender, Orden you have just walked into a minefield, if you don't surrender then we will destroy the ground you all stand on.'

Orden stopped and looked at his feet concentrating he could see a faint red glow, Orden looked to the soldiers behind him then back to Mithos.

'What would you do with us if we surrender?'

'I want you and your men to listen. I want you all to understand what your new Lord is like, how he betrayed those who trained him, about how he killed the man who raised him, then if you like we will let you all pass to join the rest of your army. You can tell your commanders what you saw and take some of the dead as proof, but I ask that you all just listen.'

'What if we refuse?' one of the soldiers asked; suddenly the ground beneath them started to glow red, they truly were stuck.

'It would be all too easy to kill you all right now.'

As the Sateran's put their swords away Mithos stepped onto the minefield and started to explain his life in the academy and what Lucian was like, focusing his mana through his vocal chords expanded the reach of his voice making sure that all of the soldiers could hear him. He described how Lucian murdered other mages he knew and had grown up with to gain more power, and how the fight went down at the academy. Mithos took a while giving Orden and the Sateran soldiers every detail involving Lucian's betrayal. When he had finished, Orden had trouble thinking what to do, looking at his men they didn't know what to think.

'Well, Orden, what are you going do?' Mithos asked still sitting in the minefield.

'I can't betray my country, but to walk away would be a betrayal. In Satera to run from an enemy is punishable by death,' Orden replied. Orden turned to his soldiers 'What do you want to do? There is only one way we can live, but it ends in betrayal.'

A soldier stepped forward, 'Sir we swore to fight for Lord Rohnal, but Lucian isn't the only one with that name, whoever wins this war will rule Satera. Whatever you decide we will follow, sir.' Mithos looked at the soldier then back to Orden.

'Decision time, Orden, will you join us, walk away, or will you fight and die?' Mithos asked.

'I don't want my men to die for nothing.' Orden drew his sword and fell to his knee, his soldiers followed his example. 'My Lord Rohnal, I die in your name, I give my life for your honour, I kill for your people to be free, by my honour and on my life, I swear my loyalty.' When the Sateran soldiers finished they all stood.

Mithos was confused by what they had said, 'What does all that mean?'

'We swear our oath of loyalty to you, it means we recognize you as our lord and master,' Orden said.

'Didn't you swear to Lucian?'

'No, we swore to his father, the previous Lord Rohnal, we haven't been sworn to Lucian Rohnal.'

Neji stepped forward, 'We need all the help we can get, Mithos adding them gives us one hundred and twenty soldiers,' Neji pointed out.

Mithos looked over the soldiers.

'Gilbert, remove the runes, dispel them, I don't want our new friends dead before we start our battle.'

Orden and the Sateran soldiers put their swords away and the village soldiers returned arrows to quivers and shouldered their bows. It took time for Gilbert to dispel the runes knowing that theses soldiers had nothing to do with the attack on the academy made it easier to accept their help. As the night crept upon them, Mithos still found it strange to have a Sateran officer riding beside him. He stopped as did the column of soldiers behind him.

'OK, we will make camp now as there are so many of us we need to set up pickets. Orden see to it.'

'Yes, my Lord,' Orden said.

As Orden organised the guards Mithos and his friends started a campfire while talking about what to do when they gather the army they needed no matter what they would have to do they would need to reach the tower before Lucian and his army.

'Mithos, Lucian said they were going to attack and destroy all the other schools right?' Ren asked as he added more wood to the fire.

'Yes, he did,' Mithos replied.

'Then shouldn't we go to the schools and warn them?'

'No need, I sent some messenger birds to every college informing them of Lucian and his plan along with a report of what happened at Manta, it won't take us long to reach the elves, we should reach them by nightfall tomorrow, we will take turns on watch. I will take the first watch Rin and Areha take the second then Neji take the third.'

'Why do you need two of us on the second watch?' Rin asked.

'Because you are weak I'm putting you with her so you don't feel left out, Neji and I are reckless that's why I haven't put you with one of us.'

'Good point, OK wake us in four hours,' Rin said as he unrolled his sleeping blanket.

Mithos watched as the soldiers put out their fires some went out on patrol the rest went to sleep. Mithos still felt unsettled by what he saw, one hundred and twenty soldiers and they were still going to gather more soldiers to form their army whilst Lucian carried out his plan to activate the towers of fate, no matter how he looked at it he would need an army to fight Lucian, but all the time it took them to gather an army that could challenge the vast legions of Satera Lucian and his chosen Mages would take the towers.

Lucian's generals gathered in the palace realm. For the Sateran generals it was their first time in a different realm and they noticed how different the air itself was. They all turned to the doors when they opened to see five people dressed in red robes with black flames

121

embroidered on them. Behind them Stood Lucian dressed in the green robes of Satera, the ancient silver marking of the Master of Satera ran up the sleeve of the green silk trench coat, his long hair showed him as a true master of Satera.

'Generals of Satera, of the vampire army and of my mages, soon the Academies of magic will be destroyed then we will be free to conquer the rest of the world, we may have a problem though, several mages from Manta have escaped and they have gone in search of aid from the elves, dark elves and the men at Nachreach, it also seems that someone has warned the Academies of what happened to Manta, any idea how that happened?'

'How do you know this, Master Rohnal?' General Sorenal asked.

'The numbers at Noventia Academy were far less then there should have been, from now on no mercy is to be shown those who do not follow me, all will be killed, that is my order, my generals Fear, Pain and Death are going to find their towers and they will need soldiers to do it, Siren and Sireen will take some Sateran soldiers to the Elvin city of Vortee, they must be conquered general's Sorenal and Gameck, you will take your soldiers with them and follow their command's, the rest of you will split into three groups and take out the last three Academies.'

After the generals organized themselves Lucian sent them all on their way. It would take some time before they could claim the towers but when all three were activated then the fourth would rise and then the world would bow before their new god.

Lucian gave maps to Death, Fear and Pain showing them the locations of their towers and the number of sacrifices they would need to activate the power of the towers. Lucian knew he could rely on Fear and Pain but

Death had always been too independent, he only joined Lucian because he was bored and there were few in his old home that could challenge him, but for the time being he was needed for Lucian's plan to succeed.

Mithos awoke to see Orden standing over a small fire, 'My Lord, I have tea brewed, would you like a cup?'

Mithos rubbed the sleep from his eyes as he sat up 'Yes thank you, Orden.' Mithos wrapped his blanket around himself as he sat by the fire with Orden. The early morning chill was slightly eased by the warm fire.

'My Lord, I was thinking it might be time to re-design the Sateran army uniform, that way we won't kill your men by mistake.'

'It is a good idea, but we have more pressing issues right now, like stopping Lucian from conquering the world, if he does many innocent people will suffer and die,' Mithos stated as he looked around to see the soldiers taking down their tents and packing up the camp and putting out fires, however, he did understand that if you don't know your own men and the enemy is in the same uniform you might kill an ally my mistake.

Chapter Twelve

Mithos and his small army march across the bridge leading to Vortee. As they cross to the land of the Elves they can see watch towers.

It wasn't surprising that the elves would make their home in such a beautiful land. The green fields were complimented by the white marble of the towers. At the top, Mithos could see the shine of steel armour, since they had been spotted it wouldn't take long for the elves to meet them and challenge their reason for being in Elvin lands. Mithos pulled his horse to a stop. His small army stopped behind him, they watched as hundreds of horses came at them from the grand city walls, the mid-morning sun made the riders' armour shine.

'Orden pull the men to a close formation,' Mithos ordered.

'Form Square,' Orden yelled. The soldiers formed a square around Mithos Orden Rin Neji and Ariha they held the formation as tight as they could whilst the Elvin Cavalry wheeled around them. They vastly outnumbered the force Mithos possessed. The Elves sat tall and proud in their saddles their armour consisted of a steel chest plate, shin guards and gauntlets, though underneath they wore black leather trousers, a shirt with a collar and gloves.

One of the Elves removed his helmet, 'What are you doing here, mage?' the Elf asked.

'We come seeking your help as your king promised the Warlocks.'

'You must be Lucian, he is the only mage that would travel with Stateran's. What say you, child?'

'I am not Lucian, he wiped out the other warlocks at Manta. I am Mithos Rohnal, my master charged me with ending Lucian's evil. We have a contract signed by your king swearing your people to lend aid to any Warlock bearing it,' Mithos said.

The elf dismounted and started to approach the Sateran wall. Mithos met him with the contract.

'May I have a closer look?' Mithos handed the contract to the elf. The looked at it as if trying to find some way out of the agreement, after a good while the elf handed the contract back. 'I see; you and your men will come with us to Vortee, we will talk more there.'

Mithos followed the elf to the stable outside the city walls. The stable was as big as a small village. The walls of Vortee seemed to reach for the sky, it must have taken thousands of years to complete. Inside the city they saw statues of Elvin soldiers carved from white marble, though it seemed all of their statues and buildings were made of the same material. The ornate carvings were on every wall, picturing great battles that the elves had been involved in over the centuries.

The soldiers led them deep into the city, the streets were full of elves, though they left a path down the centre of the road. Mithos noted the biggest building when he arrived but as they got closer it seemed larger than he originally thought, on their way to the Palace they passed shops and houses, all of them empty so they could all watch the procession of Elvin soldiers surrounding the outsiders. As they reached the Palace Mithos saw the guards dressed in gold armour, they stood to either side of the huge double doors each guard held a massive shield and a stave weapon with a large curved blade on either end. The guards stand to attention as the Elvin officer approaches.

'The Warlock will come with me, the rest can stay out here,' the officer said.

'Sorry but I can't let Master Rohnal go anywhere alone,' Orden objected.

'I agree I will stay by Mithos's side to keep him safe,' Neji added.

'No, it is a good idea, the elves wont attack any of us unless we threaten them, the rest of you stay here and stand guard,' Mithos said.

Orden and Neji looked to each other they had no choice but to agree with him. Mithos followed the officer through the halls. He had been told about the inside of the palace and the carvings, he was told that whilst they were amazing they pale in comparison to the palace in Satera, he could only imagine what they were like, they entered through an archway leading to a big room. In the centre of the room was a round table with eight chairs, in the far wall above the table was a box and inside the box was the throne. Mithos had heard of the Elvin king and how he ruled. The eight chairs round the table was where the councillors would sit to decide their laws and other political matters if they cannot come to an agreement and are locked it falls to the king to break the tie. Mithos could see the King sitting on his throne

'What is the meaning of this, Captain Morone?' the King asked.

Captain Morone went to a knee, 'Your majesty this is Mithos Rohnal, a warlock, he seeks our aid in his war against Lucian.'

The king rose from his throne, 'Is this true?'

'Yes, your majesty, your father signed the agreement – if a warlock was to come to you with the treaty you are obligated to assist with any request, and I request help from your army, your smiths and your fletchers,' Mithos said. Mithos waited for the king's response when the door under the throne box opened.

'I am king Ern, let me see the treaty.' Mithos handed the paper over to the king it seemed that all elves had a perfect complexion along with their immortality, the king looked over the paper studying it closely then finally handed it back to Mithos.

'Very well, I shall give you all the aid you require.'

'Thank you, Your Majesty.' Mithos expected it to be much more difficult to get the help they needed.

'Along with what you asked for I shall give you some information; do you know the legends of Dragons?' the king asked.

Mithos couldn't believe a topic about a mythical creature should be raised now, 'Yeah, they are fairy tale creatures, right?'

The king smiled, 'Wrong, have you ever wondered what lies south of Vortee?' the king asked.

'No one knows what lies south, we never made it that far and all ships that went there were destroyed.'

The king smiled, 'We made it south, I know what lies there, they are real and there are many types of them, they destroy any ship that comes too close to them, the marine dragons destroy them, anyone who tries to travel through our lands to reach that territory, if they survive they are killed just inside the border.'

Mithos couldn't believe the king's implication of the possible existence of Dragons, a species of creature that couldn't have lived, but Mithos didn't interrupt him. 'Dragons live far to the south some of them will be in human form, we elves were the second race to see them, the first were the Shadow Reapers who asked them to watch over a tower called the Tower of Destiny.'

Mithos's eyes widened at the name, it was the final tower Lucian would need, if Mithos could reach the tower first then he would deny Lucian what he wanted most in the world. Mithos thought on this; sending a huge force would be a mistake if the Dragons were real. Realization came over him, gathering a united army is secondary, stopping Death, Fear and Pain from activating the towers was a priority, but before he could deal with them he had to make access to the tower of destiny impossible. If the dragons really were there Mithos needed them on his side, if, however, they decided to team up with Lucian he would be able to crush any army.

'I have two Shadow Reapers with me, I can take them south and try to strike a deal with them,' Mithos said hopeful with the chance to block Lucian's advance.

'Very well, but take my son with you and a human officer. If my son is there they will not attack outright, you may leave in two days. Since you are the last student of Master Strange I will have to introduce you to someone before you leave.'

Mithos had his first powerful ally in the war, but he knew that Lucian would target them because of that.

'I will leave my men here with you and under your command whilst I am gone they will help you fend off any force Lucian sends,' Mithos added.

The night they arrived at Vortee the elves threw a massive celebration; the feasting hall was filled with music and the smell of ale and wine even though the elves were vegetarian they brought down several animals for them. The elves had no problem getting to know the humans in their care. Morone came to Mithos telling him the king wanted to see him. Morone took Mithos through the streets of Vortee. King Ern met them outside the palace.

'Morone, you may leave, this place is for the warlock's eyes only.'

Morone bowed and left them. Mithos followed the King to a secret door hidden by elfish magic making the blood of the king the only key. The way was dark, looking down there, Mithos got the feeling of foreboding there was powerful magic within the catacombs.

'Do not linger in any one place for long, keep going no matter what you may feel or see. Press on till you reach the large room at the end.'

As Mithos started inside, Ern grabbed his arm, 'You will not need your sword, in fact the magic contained within that blade will put you in danger, the magic in those halls will use it as a target and destroy you.'

Mithos couldn't understand what he meant.

'What do you mean by the magic targeting it?' Mithos asked.

'When a mage is confined unable to use his magic it escapes him, but down there it is confined, he has been down there for fifty years, the magic has become violent and will strike down any threat that, sword can't hide its power as you do.'

Mithos finally understood what he meant and removed his sword from his belt handing it to Ern to care for. As Mithos entered the hall the door closed behind him. He was trapped in complete darkness all he could do was walk through the darkness.

Orden went before the king, bowing out of respect.

'Your majesty, I know my master is on a secret quest so I won't ask what he is doing,' Orden said.

'Then what will you ask?' Orden took a piece of paper from his satchel and offered it to the king.

'How long would it take to have one hundred and twenty of them?'

'Well, if I put all of my smiths and leather workers to the task, less than a day, but I will have them make many more for you just in case more from Satera join you.'

Orden bowed before he left, happy that he would have a surprise ready for Master Rohnal upon his return.

Mithos wasn't sure how far he had walked but it seemed like the twists and turns would go on forever.

'Who goes there?' a voice said. It reminded him of the marshes were he first met the Shadow Reapers. 'Only death awaits you, retreat now,' the voice continued, but there was nowhere Mithos could go. He had to press on following the wall.

The voice wouldn't leave him alone repeating the same words over and over, 'Who goes there, only death awaits you, retreat now.'

Mithos chose to ignore the voices. Suddenly the area lit up, it looked like thousands of fire flies surrounded him, but instead of flying around they seemed to simply float, but it was the colour that amazed Mithos the most – little dots of red, yellow, blue, green, orange, purple every colour he could imagine looking around; straight ahead was the way he had to go. As Mithos stepped forward the lights began to swirl around him. 'You carry a great evil with you, it must be recognized by your eyes before you can be rid of it,' the voice said.

Mithos couldn't hold his tongue anymore.

'What evil? I seek only help!' Mithos yelled.

'The evil is part of you, it drains you of your power, it makes you weak.'

What was it on about? What evil? Surely if he carried it Master Strange would have told him, Mithos thought. Suddenly the lights started to gather creating a form, it was the same size as him. As more time passed its image became clear, it was dressed similar to a warlock, but it was white, its long hair was black as the darkness he just came from, though it wore a mask that covered it from nose to chin, yet the eyes showed it for what it was.

'I wondered how long it would be before you realized I was there,' it said.

'Who are you?' Mithos asked fearing the answer.

'You asked who I am, a simple question with a simpler answer. I am you, my name is Mithos Rohnal.'

What was this thing talking about? It must be a figment of his imagination.

'No I am not, I am part of you, my very existence is all thanks to Lucian. We are an experiment, he wants to see how powerful you could become, splitting our minds was the best way to see what part of you would prosper.' It looked down the path Mithos needed to take then smiled. 'The old fool down here will help us get rid of the other and I can't wait to be rid of you.'

Mithos followed 'It', the thing that claimed to be part of him. Mithos hadn't really noticed how far he had come, but it didn't take them long to reach the door. The other version of him reached for the door as he touched it, blue sparks covered his hand bringing to screams of pain strong enough to drop his to his knees. When the evil Mithos took his hand away Mithos touched the door, there was no pain and no sparks, he opened the door surprised to see such a huge room filled with clutter, books covered the floor, they were stacked to the ceiling they seemed to be mixed. Mithos wouldn't know where to find books on destructive spells or books on shields and words. On the left was an alchemy station and to the right were three tablets with ancient writing he couldn't read, though he recognized the symbols for fire, lightning and wind.

'Evil cannot enter this room and you can't hide your true nature from the seal on the door posts. The good one may enter unharmed.'

Mithos stepped inside the room, the air coated in the smell of old paper and dust filled his lungs, the old man on the far side of the room turned.

'I sense two souls and one body,' the evil Mithos chuckled.

'I have a body.'

'Yes, one made of mana that strayed from me.' The old man held up his hand, 'Be gone, creature,' he said. Mithos turned to his evil half, the mana that made his form disappeared in the small lights that created him. The old smiled at Mithos, though he seemed more fascinated with him. Mithos finally got a good look at his eyes, they were red, his pupils were in the shape of buzz saw blades.

'You have noticed my eyes, they allow me to see all forms of magic, they also give me insight into my enemy's spells allowing me to copy them, you can feel it can't you? I am a Rohnal, though my twin brother became the master, his magic was much stronger than mine so I moved here. That would have to be three hundred and sixty years ago.'

Mithos couldn't imagine living that long he had to be mistaken. 'How could you have lived that long?' Mithos asked.

'Since I haven't used my magic, like the elves their magic and mine have kept me alive. I fear I have only two spells left in me before I die, so why should I waste one for your sake?' the old man asked.

'Because I will die to defeat my enemy and avenge my friends and family who were murdered at Manta, one of whom was your student.'

The old man stared at him as if those red eyes were searching his soul for any hint of a lie.

'That foolish child rushing to a battle he couldn't win, I saw what happened, he sent you away because he saw the power you possess and he met the evil within. As I said, I can see the magic around you, a dividing spell, this one has the formula of the ancients, a language I know all too well, the three tablets you saw when you entered this room have the same writing, it is the reason you and that thing are separate. To balance you and give you back the power you should have had you will need to face it but if it dies then you will, too. He must be forced to submit. I will send you into your mind.'

Mithos stood in the centre of the room as the man moved his books. It seemed more like he was kicking them down. As the huge towers fell the books formed a ring around him, the old man started chanting, 'By the sacrifice of knowledge and one spell, I invoke the divines, allow this mortal to face himself, with half my life I send you to the depths of your mind.'

Mithos opened his eyes, he stood in a small green meadow, but surrounding it was a barren wasteland it was as if something was strangling the land till it withered and died.

'How long are you going to ignore me?' Mithos turned at the sound of that double voice, once again he came face to face with his evil half.

'Where are we?' Mithos asked.

'This is your mind, just look at all you have sacrificed to me already. When we split, this world was cut in half, your world and mine, now because you didn't hear my voice and relied on my power so much I have nearly taken over this world and now I have the power and opportunity to be the sole owner of this body.'

Mithos took a close look at the eyes of his evil half, they were the same as the old man's, red with that strange pupil. As Mithos stared at his evil half he didn't notice his meadow getting smaller.

'You see that it is the weakness of your mind, you will soon be part of my mind as a memory.' It drew its sword and licked the blade; it looked so sadistic. Mithos drew his sword, if this thing was his other half then it would know all his techniques. Neither of them could win, it would all come down to the unexpected.

Mithos attacked crossing to the wasteland he unleashed a flurry of attacks every slash and thrust was returned in kind, neither of them could afford to give any ground. The fight went on for what seemed like hours. Mithos noticed that the meadow started to spread the harder he fought, it was like a tug of war with the line between good and evil moving. It threw a ball of fire towards Mithos who not having time to erect a shield dived out the way.

'Why are you doing this? We are one and the same.'

It smiled, 'Because I want to be free, free to do as I please as the sole owner of this body.'

It attacked again; the wasteland began to encroach on the meadow again. Mithos finally understood how to regain his mind it wasn't going to be given he had to fight for it. Mithos gave in to his rage, he imagined everything that made him angry, he didn't need anything but his rage to give him the strength to fight.

Lucian walked through the halls of the Dragons' Palace of Satera he loved the Masters' Walk, the fine art the carvings and gems in the walls down the entire hall. There was only the throne room, the seat of power in Satera, all decisions are made by the man who sits on the throne. Lucian entered the throne room to see his messengers.

'Ben, send for the Van'wrath mistress Kelly and master Kevin,' the messenger hurried about his task running from the throne room. Lucian knew Ben would be scared to go near the quarters of the Van'wrath, but the names Kelly and Kevin added to the title scared even the bravest Sateran, in many ways they reminded him of Siren and Sireen.

Lucian sat on his throne for a while waiting before he heard their heavy boots on the marble floor as the doors opened, the light shone on the green leather they both wore a ponytail in their black hair. They stopped and made a knee as they bowed their heads.

'My Lord, what do you wish of us?' they said as one.

Lucian threw a picture at their feet one he commissioned two years ago. Kevin picked up the picture. 'That is a picture of Mithos Rohnal, he is the last of the warlocks, without him the order dies. I want you to capture him and domesticate him.'

'My Lord, I believe you have already sent Siren and Sireen to that location, why send us as well unless, unless you don't think they can beat him; that's your plan, have them weaken him and then we swoop in and capture him.'

Lucian smiled at their understanding. 'Yes, the two of them are powerful, but they will never beat him with the training he will receive with the high elves. I am sure he is getting what I could not, the power of the divine elements. Now go and be ready.'

'Master, should we take some soldiers?' Kelly asked.

Lucian found her to be quite attractive, 'Take whoever you want and when you have Mithos, Kevin, you will be left alone with him and Kelly you shall report to my quarters.' They bowed to Lucian. Though Kevin may not like the idea of someone sleeping with his sister, in this case he had no choice.

Mithos fell to his knees exhausted from the fight. He looked at his other half who seemed pleased with the fight so far, or maybe it was delighted by the cuts in Mithos's skin. How was it that Mithos hadn't even landed a single hit, not even a glancing blow? Mithos held his sword, it had been split in half, but the evil half's sword had not even a scratch or nick on its blade.

Mithos dropped his sword, it was useless, all he could do now was use his magic. Mithos thrust his hands forward losing a gale of razor winds that slashed the ground as it went howling towards it. Mithos's other half just stood there as it lifted its black sword when the wind got close it slashed downwards cutting the manna that fuelled the wind creating a gap causing the wind to pass by him. How could he win? It knew all he did and more, since Lucian cursed him the evil half seemed to retain more knowledge. Mithos's gaze returned to the broken sword, he could almost hear the spirit of his master.

'Master Strange, I need your help, how can I win?' Mithos muttered. 'Tell me is there a name you want to be called by?' Mithos asked. His other half sheathed his sword and crossed his arms as if trying to think.

'Interesting question, I am part of you, but I am different. Well, I like the name Seth, yeah that will do.'

Mithos finally had a name for him, a thought occurred to him, the headmaster shared his soul with his sword, the realization that he tried to do everything on his own washed over him like a great wave. The others offered to help him with his training but he turned them down flat out. Mithos remembered the lab in Azura when he released his rage, how could he be so stupid, he couldn't fight a war on his own, just like he couldn't defeat himself alone. Mithos rose to his feet with his jaw set with the determination to win at any cost. His sword had a soul so he would never fight alone, even if the fight was one on one his master would always fight with him.

Mithos charged towards his evil half who thinking Mithos was going for a swing blocked, but it was taken by surprise when the sword lunged forward stabbing him in the chest, it was the mortal blow to end the fight. The evil Mithos dropped to his knees clutching the blade that penetrated his heart, blood leaked around the blade and oozed from his mouth. His breathing laboured as if that simple act was taking all of his strength.

'I see you really want full control here,' it said looking up at Mithos. It was hard to see someone who looked the same as him mortally wounded.

'You win this time, but if you ever become too weak or try to use more mana, than you have then I will be back to take control.' The evil Mithos started to vanish; the last thing to go was the twisted smile the smile of one who lusts for blood.

Mithos opened his eyes, he was back in the old man's room. The old man was smiling, it was a kind smile, the type of smile Mithos always imagined a grandparent would give to a grandchild who succeeded in life. Mithos clutched his head as he fell to his knees screaming, it felt like someone was hitting the inside of his skull with a pick axe, images he couldn't recognize flooded his mind.

'Don't worry, child, the pain will pass soon, since you were split in two the spells you learnt were divided between you and the other you, but now all of the knowledge from the defeated version is pouring inside your mind,' the old man said. It seemed to take forever but the pain started to subside it came to a dull ache, it was nice to be able to think straight again.

'How do you feel?' a voice said. Mithos still couldn't see; he had no idea where the voice was coming from though he knew it was the old master.

'I feel strange and I can't see,' the panic in his own voice scared him more than he was before.

'It will pass as will the dull ache and the strange feeling you have, but for now since you are robbed of your sight, that means you must listen twice as hard.'

The old master's footsteps echoed around the room. Mithos had no idea which way he was facing, but he did know the master was behind him.

'The three divine spells are black elements fire, lightning and wind each of them carries a risk when using them; the lightning will take your sight, the wind will cut you and the fire will consume you, this happens if you are too weak or use them to many times.'

Mithos couldn't wrap his head around it, these three spells could harm and even kill him. He went over the fundamentals of magic. If you are not strong enough to use a spell it will not work, if you run out of mana your spells will not work. No matter how he thought of it the only spells that could harm the caster were blood magic, a practice that has been forbidden.

'Despite what you are thinking, they are not blood spells but divine spells; these are the last spells created by the Ancients.'

Mithos was relieved when his sight started to return but no matter how happy he was about that he had to focus on his training the three divine spells, magic that Lucian did not possess, no matter how long it took he had to learn these spells.

'What is the first step to learning these spells?' Mithos asked.

'First you need to stay where you are till your sight returns, it will give me time to right the spell forms around you, for it to work your mana form needs to be changed and for that to happen the spells need to recognize you as a potential user.'

'What do you mean they have to recognize me?'

'Unlike most spells divine spells are living spells each of them has a mind of its own, they were created from living souls, that is why they harm you with over usage, now keep quiet and let me work.'

Orden put on his new armour, it looked good, made of green steel from Satera and forged by the elves it felt light but strong looking around he saw Master Rohnal's soldiers looking like a proper army, all dressed the same, now they were ready to face the army of Lucian. Orden saw Neji on the battlements looking intently to the south. Orden started towards the battlements when he heard someone yelling.

'Scout returning, Your Majesty,' the elves moved quickly to have archers on the battlements where Neji stood. Orden and Neji stood with the king as the rider entered the city, he dismounted bowing to the king.

'Your Majesty, the dragons …'

'What about them?' the king asked.

'Sir they have been annihilated and that strange tower has been activated. It was horrible, all that was left were their bones.'

Orden and Neji looked to each other.

'Did you see anyone near the tower?' Neji asked.

'No, sir, if someone was there they would have been inside the tower,' the scout replied.

Another soldier called out, 'Scout returning from the northwest.'

Orden and Neji ran with the king to the north gate, they met up with Areha, Gilbert and Rin as the rider entered the gate.

'Your Majesty, an army approaches from the north.'

'How far out?' Orden asked. 'About a day's march, sir.' the scout replied as he dismounted.

Orden, Neji, Gilbert, Areha and Rin met king Ern in the war room, they had to come up with a battle plan once they had a full report on what the scout saw. The scout read out his report so they could all hear.

'An army of around five hundred thousand soldiers are marching towards us, two people one male and one female dressed in red coats with black flames rode at the head of the army, they move at a slow and steady pace and should arrive in roughly twenty-four hours, this ends my report.' The scout stood to attention. Whilst they thought about the information King Ern turned to Orden.

'What would you say is the best way to fight a Sateran force?' the king asked.

'How many soldiers do you have?' Orden asked.

'Ten thousand in this city, it would take far too long to gather any more from other Elvin lands.'

'In that case the best way would be to take out the officers and NCOs destroying their chain of command.'

King Ern thought about it for a while, 'Why is that so important, they already know what to do, I mean surely they have been given orders to destroy us?'

'No, only the officers are given orders on where they are to attack. Lucian wants the magic contained here so he won't hit us too hard. They will focus at certain points.'

Ern had one of the soldiers bring a map of the city so they could look for points where Lucian would have the Sateran soldiers attack. Ern pointed out the library where books on Elvin magic were kept as well as the door that led to the catacombs under the city where Mithos was.

'Do you have a map of the catacombs and any other entrances to where Mithos was?' Gilbert asked.

'No there isn't, what lies down there is too important for any record of its layout to be kept,' King Ern replied.

Orden, Rin, Ariha and Neji stared at the map. 'The north is the best place for an attack since the door and library were located in the south of the city,' Neji said.

'I agree; though they may send a small contingent to the south in order to make us think they will perform an attack on both fronts, so it might be a good idea to have a few archers at the southern wall. The northern route is also the weakest point since most dangers come from the east west and the south where the dragons were.'

Chapter Thirteen

Since they had chosen the best places to defend they had to talk about the possibility of asking some close allies for reinforcements, but every idea was shot down, the only army close enough was the dark Elves, but they hated the high Elves, they would rather see them butchered than rush to their aid.

'Gilbert, does it have to be a member of the warlocks to deliver that message?' Neji asked.

'We might be able to send a messenger if we could send proof with them that they did not steal it,' Gilbert replied.

'Then send Rin and give him your pendant, he has magic to prove it was one from Manta that sent him and the pendant will be further proof that he was sent by a warlock.'

They all turned to look at Rin.

'It will take you two days to get there and back, they might take another day to get their army together, you will arrive two days after they start their attack,' Orden said. Rin gathered a bag of food for his trip, Gilbert handed the treaty agreement and pendant over as an Elf approached with a horse and gave the reins to Rin. Once he mounted his steed, King Ern, Orden and Gilbert approached him.

'Remember stop for nothing and keep heading east no matter what you see or hear,' Orden reminded him. With a slap to the horse's rump they sent Rin on his way.

Mithos opened his eyes, his sight had returned fixing his gaze to the floor he saw that he was in the centre of a chalk circle, there were five rings to the circle that were broken in three places those sections had the symbols for fire, wind and lightning, the inscriptions inside the five rings were in an ancient tongue that he didn't know, but he felt uneasy at seeing how harsh they looked, as if they were a curse.

'Master, what does that writing mean?' Mithos asked unable to shake the fear from his voice.

'Each one is a prayer. Look at the symbol for fire, it starts there and goes round to the right, they symbolize your effort to protect the magic in the world from those who seek to destroy or misuse it. If you break your vow and misuse magic then the black flame will consume you. As I said before, the three spells are alive with minds and souls of their own, they were the first spells the gods gave us, along with these spells special instructions were passed down, all life is magic something special to protect, these spells are bestowed on the chosen guardians of life. As soon as I finish this spell you and I will be the last, as the others died without naming an heir as will you, these spells should be lost to history that is why I didn't teach them to my last student your headmaster, but Lucian, being as powerful as he is, I think that only one of these spells will be able to touch him at this point, you will be given these spells and their protection but not the knowledge on how to pass them on, that is why I wrote them when you were blind, so you couldn't know how I wrote them. If you try to pass it on and write them the wrong way the spells will kill both you and whoever you try to pass them on to. Now do you agree to protect life and the purity of magic?'

Mithos took a deep breath, 'Yes I do.'

The old master wove five hand signs, as he finished the last hand sign the three symbols started to glow as if they were rune mines, but as quick as they started to glow they turned black, the writing around them started to turn within the circle. As the speed of their rotation quickened the words started to rise from the ground, the inner circle stopped at his feet the other four stopped around other parts of his body with the outer circle stopping at eye level. The rotation seemed to keep getting faster and faster and as the speed increased Mithos could have sworn he heard a voice as if it was in a distant place. Mithos felt the strong urge to close his eyes so he could focus on the voice, the voice started to get stronger, from a faint whisper to a booming deep commanding voice.

'Hear my name, mortal, engrave it in your heart and mind and I shall bestow upon you the black elements. I am the god of fire and war, Marik.' The voice's words seemed to burn Mithos's flesh. His eyes arms and legs felt like they were on fire, it was as if the name itself would melt his skin away and the voice would grind his bones to dust. Mithos was forced to his knees by the voice.

'Speak my name,' the voice commanded. Mithos felt himself gasping for air he couldn't allow himself to fail here.

'It was a simple ritual you have been through things like this before,' he lied to himself.

'As you command, Lord Marik.'

Suddenly he was enveloped in flames and lightning. Mithos closed his eyes expecting pain but it never came he slowly reopened his eyes, the elements weren't just around him they were coming from him, the fire felt warm, not hot, almost like a coat protecting him from the chill. Mithos looked at the old man.

'Is that it?'

The old man smiled, 'Not yet, you have the spells but now you need to learn to control them otherwise they will be useless to you in battle and don't forget if you push yourself too hard and run too low on mana the other you will take over and the last thing we need is that loose cannon on the battlefield.'

Neji joined Orden on the battlements he could hear the rumbling of formation marches in the distance.

'Are you nervous, Orden,' Neji asked.

'Yes, this is the first big battle I have been in,' Orden replied.

Neji looked out to the plain, 'This is where they will attack, a lot of people will die and if you let it weigh on your mind you will be among them sooner or later.' Neji caught sight of a light out on the plain.

'What is it?' Orden asked. Neji's eyes opened wide with sudden realization it was the fire of a torch.

'Orden sound the alarm the enemy is here.'

The elves and free Sateran's as they called themselves started rushing about getting to their posts ready for battle. King Ern joined Neji and Orden 'what is going on?' Ern asked between gasping breaths.

'Our information was wrong the enemy is here I think they are getting ready to lose a volley of fire arrows. Pass the message along to duck below the battlements and ready arrows.'

The message was passed along. As the field filled with dots of light soon a hail of arrows came down on the city. Just as Neji said, they were fire arrows. Neji peeked through the slit in the battlements, he saw a second wave of arrows take flight, as the second volley of arrows hit the buildings and ground Neji saw the elves had their bows ready to fire. Seeing the enemy were still loading Neji gave the signal to open fire the archers one after the other fired as the next elf had fired the first was ready to fire again. They could hear the screams as the arrows hit their target. The elves kept shooting it seemed they were aiming for the ones who loaded the fire arrows but there were so many more Sateran soldiers than they had archers and every Sateran could use a bow.

Despite having fewer soldiers they were able to take down many of the enemy. It wasn't long before the sun started to rise and they could see the enemy. It revealed two people walking between two lines of soldiers. The look on gilbert's face showed why the shields and mines didn't work. The red coats with black flames echoed the thought.

'Gilbert, are they the twins?' Neji asked.

'Yes and my magic is nothing compared to them.'

The male held out his hand sending a shockwave of air that destroyed the gate. The Elvin archers squatted aiming their arrows inside the city as the Sateran soldiers poured through the gates meeting the free Sateran soldiers right at the entrance. It was a sea of green smashing against a small red river, though a river with a strong current with the shields given to them by the elves they stopped the green Sateran's from getting through the gates. The fact that Siren didn't destroy the entire wall worked against his army since it worked as a funnel with the wall still intact numbers were taken out of the equation. Orden had his soldiers stand firm as the enemy crashed into the shields trying to push them back, but the free Sateran soldiers were packed too tight together more and more of Lucian's men smacked into the battering ram of men.

'Now!' Orden yelled. On that word the soldiers holding the shields pushed them to the side and the soldiers in the second line lunged forward with spears. Screams of pain filled the air as the spear points pierced chests stomachs and limbs. As the weapons were pulled back the shield holders brought them back smashing the skulls of the next line of soldiers. As the tactic had already been used they changed to strategy two – the spike wall – the shields were in such a place that there was a hole between each soldier as the enemy came too close the second line thrust their spears forward through the holes. Line after line was skewered like a stuck pig, building a new wall of dead flesh. After ten lines had fallen, when the man in a red trench coat approached, the woman walked just behind him as he stretched out his hand. The free Sateran's moved back with the man's power; it was the best move, though really it was like a choice of when you wanted to die.

Lucian's soldiers poured through the gate as they came into sight, the elves opened fire upon them the ones the arrows missed were met by free Sateran blades, the elves were soon out of arrows, freeing the enemy of death from above but the elves drew their swords, taking two steps forward they dropped with the tips of their swords aiming for the heads of the enemy as they landed their swords punched holes in the enemy's skulls and the force of the blows made their brains gush out.

The city erupted into a battlefield, the sounds of clashing steel, battle cry's and screams of death. Orden Gilbert, Neji and Ariha stayed together cutting down any enemy that came too close. They weren't looking for soldiers they wanted the two generals they looked up at the battlements there they stood their red coats billowing in the wind the black flames on their coats looked like real fire. Gilbert ran up the steps to the battlements and came face to face with Siren and Sireen the two traitors who

147

helped Lucian destroy the academy and kill their friends 'Looky what we have here, sis, the born fool who messes up every spell he tries,' Siren mocked. Sireen giggled.

'Who knows, maybe he can actually tie his shoe laces now without falling on his rump,' She added to her brother's insult. Gilbert threw out his hand in a fit of anger launching a ball of fire at them the ball exploded on contact, as the dust from the explosion started to clear the twins were still laughing. Siren had his arms crossed and Sireen had hers on her hips the wall around them was gone but they remained unscathed, untouched by the fire. The twins opened their coats showing their swords they both wore two short swords that they drew with their thumbs facing the hilt, they held the swords with the blades running up their forearms.

'Will you not use your magic against us?' Gilbert asked.

The twins simply smiled as they slowly approached, 'We want to save our mana for when we find Mithos, till he arrives you will entertain us,' they said as one.

Neji and Ariha drew their swords and black marks appeared around their eyes. Their green eyes turned black focusing their vision, the two Shadow Reapers were prepared to do what they had trained for over a thousand years of single combat. They charged the twins lunging for them, the twins turned to face each other, they were never apart so their combat style was that of a mirror. As Neji and Ariha swung and thrust their swords the twins made simple movements so the blades barely missed them, Gilbert knew it was the way they liked to fight to prove to their enemies that together they were almost invincible with magic and steel. They finally turned one of their swords to fight Gilbert and Orden joined in the fight. The twins dodged and blocked every sword swing, it seemed like sport to them. Having had enough of the game, Sireen stabbed her sword in Orden's left calf; pain took Orden to his knee as Sireen slowly twisted the blade in Orden's leg. The others tried to help their friend, but Siren kept getting in their way, she got in a few slashes of her own, they were only shallow cuts but they were numerous and they really stung. Sireen seemed to realize her other sword was far too clean for her liking, she jammed the blade into Orden's other leg through the upper thigh, repeating what she had done to his calf. Orden fought through the pain and twisted his body bringing his sword round aiming for Siren's neck. Drawing the swords from Orden's legs Sireen backed off standing beside his sister. Orden lay on his side since his legs could no longer support his weight. Gilbert had seen them fight before and knew that the twins were simply playing with them; if the twins wanted they could have put them all down minutes ago, but he also knew they wouldn't kill till they had had their fun.

Mithos formed the flame in his hand, the black flame started to give off an aura of black lightning, the old master circled him smiling at his progress.

'Now, child, add the wind and turn the fire and lightning,' the old master said.

Mithos used his left hand to add the wind and slowly the fire started to turn, the speed increased getting faster and faster till he held a hurricane made of fire and lightning.

'That will do, child.'

Mithos let the mana go and the spell faded.

'You may now leave and help our army. But first you will have my last gift.'

'What gift?' Mithos asked.

'I am old and dying, I would like you to have my mind, I will merge my mind with yours and live in your subconscious that way I will be able to give you advice in battle.'

Mithos wasn't sure what to say. 'Ha-how would you do it, how is it even possible?'

The old man smiled, 'Like this,' he said as he put his fingers either side of Mithos's head. Mithos let out a scream as the old man's fingers sunk in to his head, after two white flashes the old man crumpled to the floor.

Mithos checked the old master's pulse he was dead.

'I'm not dead, you idiot,' a voice said. Mithos looked around to see no one. 'I'm in your head, moron, now hurry up and get your backside topside whilst you still have an army.'

The image of soldiers fighting flashed through Mithos's mind. He ran down the dark hall running as fast as he could. It didn't take long for him to reach the door. Using a blast of air the door exploded into little more than splinters, out in the city Mithos heard battle cries as well as the sound of metal clashing. He felt magic in the air; it was thick with it. Following the trail of magic Mithos saw the city filled with soldiers fighting, and on one of the battlements he saw two people who made his blood boil – Siren and Sireen.

Mithos saw a bucket of water he dipped both hands in the bucket then, as Siren taught him, he aimed three fingers entwining the water drops with some of his mana. Mithos fired six droplets at them sending them flying faster than an arrow they seemed to sense the mana approaching and blocked them with their swords.

Siren and Sireen turned from their toys to look at the one they had been waiting for using the weapon they had taught him. They watched as he ran through the battlefield, cutting down every Sateran he saw wearing green. As he reached the top of the battlements he chopped the air with both hands sending blades of water flying towards them. Mithos drew his sword and started walking towards them. Siren and Sireen backed away from Mithos's friends and it didn't take long for him to get between them, looking over his shoulder, Mithos saw that Orden was badly wounded and the others were covered in cuts.

'Gilbert, heal Orden, then the two of you and Neji go and join the battle, Ariha you stay here and watch my back, kill any enemy soldier that gets too close to me.'

Gilbert quickly made to heal Orden, but the others were concerned. Mithos focused his mana to the bottom of his feet and burst into a dead run slashing towards the twins, the twins dodged and parried every swing of his sword, but they couldn't do much other than block and dodge. Mithos thrust his hand forward sending a ball of liquid fire at them quickly followed by two slashes of air, they threw out shields of spirit magic the only thing that could ward air

Siren sheathed his sword before he let loose his attack throwing out spirit whips, they snaked along the ground to try and net him, but Mithos infused his sword with Spirit magic, swinging the blade and sending a sharp shockwave of Spirit magic that cut the snaking tendrils of spirit whips. Mithos couldn't be happier that he was trained by Lucian in a fight like this, he would have been long dead if he wasn't.

Siren drew his swords again charging full force towards Mithos. Mithos sheathed his sword, he finally had him, Sireen thought. Suddenly Mithos vanished for a second, reappearing behind her brother and thrusting out a hand a bolt of black lightning emerged from Siren's chest.

Sireen could feel her legs shake as she saw the hole in his chest, her brother fell to his knees.

'What are you?' Siren asked realizing what had happened to him. Suddenly he was consumed in black fire, in seconds he was reduced to ash. Mithos turned to Sireen his vision was weak and it felt like he had water in his ears. He drew his sword preparing to receive an attack but then he saw the tears falling down her cheeks. Mithos didn't back down, Sireen looked over the battle then back to Mithos, she parted her lips and sent a deafening scream which changed to a shockwave knocking them all over. Mithos sprawled on the floor, saw Sireen draw her sword, there was murderous rage in her eyes.

Sireen charged towards Mithos, she was ready to kill him. Quick as a flash, Orden moved and jammed a knife in her leg, Sireen screamed, this time in pain, she kicked Orden and ripped the knife from her leg, throwing it to the floor she turned to run. Mithos crawled to the edge of the battlements and saw the dark elves smashing into the enemy, Mithos let a smile come to his face the fight was all but over. Yet looking at the dead he felt an ach in his heart for the pointless loss of life over what? – one man's lust for power. Mithos clenched his teeth.

'Magic, it is all because of magic, all this death just because someone wanted more magical power, wanted to become a god,' his friends all looked to each other then down at the floor.

Mithos's gaze took in the soldiers again. Lucian's troops had surrendered, they had had enough of the fighting and could see they had already lost.

A man stepped forward, 'Will you accept our surrender?'

Mithos stared at the man. 'Yes and if you like you can join our forces; we aim to free Satera and all other lands from Lucian and his Evil servants.'

The Sateran soldiers dropped to their knees. 'Lord Rohnal, we swear our loyalty our lives and our honour to you, long live Satera. Long live Lord Rohnal!' they said as one.

When everyone joined in the cheers Mithos felt weak and collapsed then everything went dark.

Chapter Fourteen

Mithos opened his eyes he felt so tired his full vision and hearing had returned though his legs ached he found that his wrists did as well he looked up since his wrists were held tight he was in a small stone room opposite his was a table with two chairs, two chairs with two people sitting in them, both blond, the man had blue eyes and the woman had green, they both wore black and green leather outfits, at their hips they wore a foot long silver spike.

'Well, well, look who's up, Kevin,' the woman smiled as the man stood.

'Oh my, I believe you are correct, Kelly. It took three days, but he has finally come out to play,' Kevin said. The sinister grin on his face made Mithos's stomach turn.

The one named Kevin drew the Silver Spike. 'Do you know what this is?' Kevin asked. Mithos shook his head. 'It is called a Naseen chord, it means blood lesion, we are called Van'wrath, that means soul teacher in the old tongue.' Kevin grasped both ends of the spike and drew a thin blade from it. 'You will learn to fear this more than any other type of magic. Allow me to show you.' Kevin drew the blade across Mithos's chest barely enough to scratch him, but the pain exploded through him. It was like every nerve suddenly caught fire. Mithos gasped as Kevin removed the blade but the pain only dimmed. 'The slightest touch from a Naseen chord will bring you pain and the deeper you are cut the worse the pain becomes, Lord Rohnal has permitted me to tell you a few things first. Nachreach has already been conquered and the friends you have sent there have already been killed and soon enough those traitors that you have gathered along with the elves will all die.'

Mithos felt the rage wash over him he tried to summon the divine spells to rip these two apart, but nothing happened no black wind no black lightning and no black fire. Mithos's eyes opened wide in realization he couldn't feel his mana, this was wrong he should feel the power there in the centre of his being, but it wasn't there. How could it not be there? What had these people done to him? Mithos thought.

Kevin had returned his Naseen chord to its spike he pulled on the tip of the spike and pulled a long section of wire from it.

'Now your lesion begins.'

Mithos felt the sting of the whip before the burning pain of the Naseen Chord sank in. Kevin seemed to enjoy giving pain. He loved to shed blood. When he eased up, Mithos took the opportunity to speak.

'Why are you doing this?' Kevin and Kelly looked at him as if he was daft.

'Because those are our orders, Lord Rohnal told us to do it so we do it, it is as simple as that,' Kelly said from her tone to these two it is like a carrier that they take pride in. Mithos felt another lash of the whip followed by the searing pain of the magic, for some reason it felt worse this time, the lash sting stopped but the burning pain didn't, in fact it got worse, the pain grew every second.

Mithos thought he would pass out but he didn't he wished he would since it would stop the pain.

'Oh, did we forget to tell you, when we drink a small amount of your blood it gives us control over your power and your mind. To an extent we can stop you from passing out and compel you to do what we want. The compulsion combined with the torture breaks your will,' Kelly said.

'So you can see how futile it is yes? Sooner or later you will do what we say the more you fight us the more pain you will bring upon yourself,' Kevin added.

Kelly left the room leaving Mithos alone with Kevin the one who had done all the work so far. Kevin jammed the Naseen chord in Mithos's leg till the spike's point protruded from the other side of the leg. Kevin pressed a button on the other end it suddenly felt like a thousand tiny blades cut into the muscle of his leg. Kevin put his mouth close to Mithos's ear.

'Allow me to explain a little more about the Naseen chord. The magic of the weapon is fused with the Van'wrath who wields it. So I can turn the pain on and off at will.'

Mithos felt the burning pain explode in his leg, it was like the pain radiated from tiny blades going in every direction. Mithos thought it would break his bones he wasn't sure it didn't.

'The button I pressed opened the two thousand tiny blades that run down the length of the shaft. Now Swear your life to Lord Rohnal and you will feel no more pain. Remember, I know your mind so if you don't mean it then I will know.'

Mithos worked up some saliva and spat in Kevin's face. 'Go to the underworld asshole.'

Kevin wiped the spit from his face and smiled. 'Oh, you will be fun, I will teach you many things about my kind, our powers and about yourself.'

Kevin wove a hand sign causing his hand to glow green, he placed it on Mithos's shoulder, he heard a sickening crack as the bone popped from its socket Mithos screamed in agony, this seemed worse than the Naseen chord, as if the pain snaked down his arm rattling his bones.

'Mithos you need to act fast, there is no way you can escape at the moment, so you must lock away your sanity and your strength of will, I will help you, they must be locked with me,' Master Rohnal said.

Mithos had no choice, he gave over his will and his sanity to the old master's care and then he was truly alone with Kevin.

After three hours with Kevin Kelly came back and Kevin left, but before he left he whispered in Mithos's ear, 'I promise you this, just because she is a woman don't think she will go easy on you. By the end of the next six hours you will want me to work on you.'

Mithos soon realized how correct Kevin had been. Kelly's technique involved less blood, but far more pain and she had not even drawn the Naseen chord yet. They both used a strange form of magic that did strange things. Kelly spent a good hour slowly boiling his blood it was a new lesson in pain, he could feel it under his skin and in his chest. After the six hours were up Kevin returned. When he saw Mithos Kevin smiled as if to admire Kelly's work. She turned to him. It seemed like she looked disappointed.

'It's over already, but I was just starting to have fun,' Kelly said. Kevin walked up to the chain that was attached to Mithos's wrist restraints and pulled it till Mithos's toes barely brushed the floor. The restraints cut into his wrists.

'Now you spat at me today, so you will spend the night like this with our Naseen chords in your legs. You

157

will be left with the pain till we wake up. When we do, if you behave, we might feed you.'

Kevin and Kelly left him to hang with the agony of the Naseen chords flowing through him, the pain was constantly changing striking bone muscle his blood and organs.

Mithos wanted to pass out but the magic didn't allow him to. True to his word Kevin and Kelly left him hanging all night. He couldn't sleep the pain wouldn't allow it he wanted to pass out from the pain but the magic wouldn't allow it. The first rays of sunlight came through the small window opposite him, but it was a good while before they came to see him. Mithos expected them to push the button so the blades would retract, but they didn't. Kelly simply pulled it out and the blades ripped through his leg. Kevin twisted his Naseen chord as he removed it. They waved the blood-soaked weapons in front of him showing him the blade-covered spike. Finally, they pushed the buttons to retract the blades.

'It is time for breakfast. Now will you do as we command?' Kevin asked Mithos not having eaten the past couple of days he nodded. Kevin released the chain letting Mithos slump to the floor. Kelly took out a silver collar with a silver chain attached, 'Put it round your neck,' she commanded. Mithos did what she said and clipped it in place. 'Now there is only one way to remove it and that is for one of us to do it or for both of us to die. Kelly unlocked Mithos's wrists as Kevin attached a sword to his left hip.

Kelly pulled Mithos along by the chain she chatted with Kevin, their hair was held in a ponytail Kevin's was slick with oils, as they walked through the halls Mithos saw Sateran soldiers guarding doors and patrolling the halls, as Kevin and Kelly passed them the guards bowed their heads. It didn't take long before Mithos saw others dressed the same as Kevin and Kelly. They must have been Van'wrath. Mithos counted ten including these two.

They finally came to a set of double doors with a servant in front of them, the servant pushed open the double doors and Mithos took in something horrifying – there had to be at least fifty Van'wrath, sixty there were sixty Van'wrath at least. Mithos could see some of them had prisoners of their own Kevin and Kelly sat. Kevin turned to Mithos and clicked his fingers and pointed at the floor. Mithos took the hint and sat on the floor with his legs crossed. Two people walked up to them with two plates filled with bacon, black pudding, sausages, mushrooms, fried eggs and beans. One of them held a small bowl. The servants put the plates on the table and waited for Kevin to nod before placing the bowl on the floor. It was filled with some grey gruel. But having not eaten for three days Mithos would have eaten anything, even the lumpy-water-based gruel. After Kevin and Kelly had finished their breakfast, Kevin picked up an apple and Mithos's chain once Kevin gave it a tug and Mithos stood, it was like he could feel the tingle of magic forcing him to do as ordered. Mithos was led back to the room, he had to admit the walk to breakfast was enjoyable compared to the torture to come, he almost wished to go for another walk.

Kevin put Mithos back in the restraints and raised him to the point where he had to stay on his toes. Kevin wove a hand sign, a blood red glow came round his hands. Kevin pressed a glowing finger to Mithos's shoulder. This pain was worse than the full six hour session with Kelly. Kevin put his third finger to Mithos's shoulder, the pain grew, Mithos could feel blood filling his mouth as Kevin moved the fingers to his throat. When Kevin removed his fingers Mithos was able to spit out the frothing blood, gasping for breath.

'As you can see I know how to cause more pain than Kelly. You will soon learn that she is kind compared to me, you will wish for her private sessions,' Kevin said. As he placed the palm of his hand on Mithos's chest it felt like his heart was being ripped out through his rib cage. Every breath was a new lesson in pain. When Kevin removed his hand, Mithos didn't have the strength to stay on his feet. When he let his weight drop the restraints started to cut his wrists again; blood dripped from the cuffs round his wrists.

Chapter Fifteen

'Where is he?' Mathew said. He had only just arrived in the Elvin city. Apparently Mithos went missing a week ago and no one could find him. From what he had been told one out of twenty guards survived the attack, but from what he had heard no one had heard a sound and the guard didn't have the chance to draw his sword.

'I'm telling you it was the Van'wrath, they are the only ones who can pull it off, he has to be in Satera,' Orden said.

'No one doubts you, but we must be sure,' Neji said as he tried to calm Orden. Areha wasn't much better, they had to restrain her to stop her from grabbing every weapon and going out alone.

As they waited, an Elf woman came out of the hospice.

'He is awake but dying, there is nothing we can do.'

Mathew, Orden and Sara entered the hospice, the guard was awake. 'Captain I saw Van'wrath, they captured Lord Rohnal,' the man said.

'Easy, soldier, calm yourself and tell us what you saw,' Orden said.

'Yes, sir. Two people, a man and a woman, both had blond hair and were dressed in green leather outfits with black trench coats bearing the insignia of the house of

Rohnal.' When the soldier was done speaking he let out his last breath never to draw another. Orden turned to Mathew.

'Gather every soldier in the united army, we march for Satera in one hour,' Orden said.

Mathew sat on the battlements how could they do this, take the most important man, the leader of their army and the last true Warlock? Areha came to sit next to him.

'We will get him back,' she said.

'You have feelings for him, don't you?' Mathew said.

Areha simply nodded. Mathew had to admit a little jealousy over that, along with confusion. She was a Shadow Reaper, they were supposed to have no emotion, maybe she had spent too long with Mithos.

Mathew looked out on the land where the army gathered. Every high elf and dark elf along with the Saterans who changed sides and the few soldiers Mathew was able to find in Nachreach. It wasn't much compared to the Sateran army along with all the monsters Lucian had gathered.

'Mithos has been captured he is the most powerful mage I know, even stronger than Master Strange of the warlocks. He was taken by the Van'wrath to Satera, so we will go to Satera and lay siege to their capital city.'

The army gave out a mighty cheer whilst they pumped their fists into the air. Mathew ran down the steps from the battlements and mounted his horse and led the march to Satera.

When Mithos woke he found himself on the floor. Only one of his eyes would open and the broken ribs made it hard to breath. Each breath was a new lesson in pain; he wasn't sure how he ended up on the floor. Master Kevin always hung him by his wrists. He saw the door open, Kevin and Kelly entered the room. Mithos rolled over on his hands and knees head bowed.

'Master, Mistress welcome home,' Mithos said. He learnt all too well that not being polite to them would result in a kick to his broken ribs.

Kevin smiled, 'Lay down and rest for a while longer, you will need your strength for what I have planned.'

Mithos felt so weak; they only fed him enough to keep him alive and he was only allowed an hour or two of sleep. Almost every night he was left hanging with a different spell over him.

Mithos would take any chance he got to sleep; he was so tired he started to get headaches, he had lost track of time in this place. He was sometimes scared to sleep because it meant being woke by a boot to his face it only made the pain in his head worse. Mithos woke up and heard Kevin and Kelly talking, 'Are you sure he is ready, Kevin, you know what will happen if we are wrong,' Kelly said. She seemed concerned.

'Well then we will just have to test him won't we and if he fails then we get tough on him removing his food and sleep privileges.' Kevin kicked Mithos's head in the usual way he woke him. 'What is your name boy?' Kevin asked.

'I am Mithos Rohnal,' Mithos answered.

'Who do you serve?' Kelly asked.

'I serve Master Kevin and Mistress Kelly of the Van'wrath.'

They looked to each other and smiled. 'It is time we will take him to Lord Rohnal,' Kevin said.

Kevin and Kelly pulled Mithos along by the chain. They walked through the halls as normal. When the soldiers saw Kevin and Kelly they bowed as the Van'wrath passed them. They came to a hall that looked bigger than the others, the stone used in the halls had carvings of dragons and symbols of magic, some of the magic symbols were instructions on ancient and lost spells. Mithos recognized the language from some of his lessons with Lucian. They finally stopped outside huge gilded double doors. Both of the doors had pictures of dragons fighting. Kevin opened the door, it opened up to a courtyard there was a stone tower in the centre, it was huge, bigger than anything Mithos had seen in his life.

Mithos followed Kevin and Kelly round the tower to the entrance where there were three people in red robes with black flames on them. For a long time neither the three men nor the two Van'wrath moved. They were expecting each other to bow, but none of them would back down.

'We will take it from here,' one of the men said in a deep voice. Mithos thought that these men had the strangest hair colour he had ever seen, the one with the deep voice had red hair and his eyes were orange, one of the others had blue hair and his eyes were blood red with a strange pattern that looked like a buzz saw blade, it seemed to spark a memory he had seen those eyes before.

Mithos was pulled from his thoughts when the man with blue hair spoke up. 'Pain that is enough, our orders are to escort them to him. Both Kevin and Kelly are needed for their pet to pledge loyalty to lord Lucian.' His voice was softer almost quiet but void of emotion.

Mithos followed the five of them up the stairs in the tower, with Kelly holding his chain of course. It took a half hour to reach the top of the stairs but when they arrived Mithos found himself in a huge room with only one window that overlooked the whole city and miles around the city. A man stood in front of the window, he wore the same robes as the three men however he wore it open to reveal Warlock's clothing. Mithos had no doubt that this was Lucian.

'Mithos, my old student it is a pleasure to finally see you again.' Mithos saw everyone else fall to a knee and started to follow when he heard a voice in his head. 'Don't do it,' the voice said. He thought it sounded familiar almost like the eyes of the man with blue hair. Kevin stood and walked behind Mithos he drew his Naseen chord placing it on the back of Mithos's neck the pain brought him to his knees.

'It is a pleasure to see you again, Lord Rohnal,' Mithos said.

Lucian turned to the window, 'It seems his army has arrived. Fear, go to the front lines, Pain, join with the second line of defence, Death wait outside, kill anyone who comes to close to the tower.' The three men bowed and left the tower leaving Mithos alone with Lucian Kevin and Kelly.

'Now, Mithos I need your help; this tower will only activate with a powerful mage in the seat and the sacrifice of a powerful mage who is loyal to the one in the chair – are you loyal, my boy?' Lucian asked.

'Yes my—'

'Don't be a fool, Mithos,' the voice said and like a jolt of lightning suddenly he remembered everything: who he was, what his mission was and who he had to kill.

'Well, my pet, answer Lord Rohnal,' Kelly ordered.

Mithos looked to her then back to Lucian. 'You will die, Lucian!' Mithos yelled.

Kevin went to stab Mithos in the leg, but missed as Mithos hit him with a spinning back kick. Kelly tried to stop Mithos by boiling his blood the pain caught his breath in his throat as he dropped to his knees.

When the tower shook, Kelly's concentration dropped, the pain that crippled Mithos eased enough for him to stand. Mithos picked up Kevin's Naseen chord and rammed the point of the spike through her throat. Mithos drew Kelly's Naseen chord, after spending weeks under the weapon he knew how it could be used. Mithos drew the blade from the spike, surprisingly he felt the pain from the weapon. His glare fixed on Lucian, Mithos charged at him. He finally had his enemy the man who betrayed them and killed mages they had both known their entire lives.

Mithos was shocked when he passed through Lucian. It was a projection so he couldn't attack or be attacked. Mithos knew this was powerful magic.

'That was a good try, but I thought this might happen,' the projection said. 'Your army is quite formidable but when you are dead I will be free to kill them all and find another mage to sacrifice.'

The roof of the tower started to change, it turned into a spiral staircase around the outside of the room.

'Meet me on the roof and we will finish this,' the projection said before vanishing. Mithos felt around the collar and found a small hole. He reached round with the Naseen chord and put the tip of the spike in the hole, the collar clicked before it fell to the floor.

Mithos climbed the stairs to the roof of the tower the opening closed behind him and there he was, Lucian standing in front of an altar. Mithos saw his sword lying on the roof just at his feet. Mithos bent down to pick it up. 'You have come far to withstand the pain of the Naseen chord and overcome the hold of the Van'wrath Kevin and Kelly, very impressive, my boy.'

Mithos started to walk towards Lucian soon enough they would start fighting and one of them would die more than likely both of them would die.

'Tell me why you did this, I want the truth,' Mithos said.

'The truth? Well, I want to be a god, plain and simple, the old gods have abandoned mankind so I will use the magic of the towers to become a god and rule over this world, can't you see it, a world without murder without war, theft and rape? I will force all people to obey my laws as the ruler of Satera and the god of this world.'

This was madness, Mithos thought, 'So you will kill all who don't bow to your wishes, don't you see that is slavery? What are we without free will if not slaves? What about the people who kill in self-defence, will they be guilty too?'

'Yes, that is just an excuse, only a god can judge man and I will be that one,' Lucian replied.

Mithos drew his sword and touched his power it was good to feel it again, to know that his defence was there and this time it would stay there. Mithos buckled the sword to his belt and started to summon his magic calling it forth as he always did before, Mithos unleashed a huge ball of ice it was a slow moving spell but powerful; if it touched Lucian it would kill him. Mithos wove the hand signs for access to faster magic.

As the ice ball dissipated Mithos threw a barrage of fire blasts at Lucian, as each ball of flame got close enough Mithos could see a shield, it was a double layered reinforced shield, it would take a lot of mana to break through the first shield and the second would drain the rest. He had to think of a way around it.

Mithos readied his sword and using the black wind dashed towards Lucian with one swing he smashed through the first shield and then the second with a second swing, his third strike was blocked with Lucian's own sword. Mithos jumped back the rarest fights were those of mages with swords.

Every slash and thrust Mithos made was blocked or dodged by Lucian. Mithos did the same, if they got close enough they poured magic into their hands, it was a basic form of combat but effective without expending too much mana. Mithos gripped his sword in both hands and with all his force he broke the blade of Lucian's sword. Lucian spun and hit the nerve in Mithos's arm with his index and middle fingers forcing him to drop his own sword. Lucian backed off weaving hand signs and chanting. Mithos knew it was a summoning spell. Mithos needed to hurry; he started his own spell.

Mithos finished his summoning a few seconds after Lucian. It was strange to see Lucian's red dragon again this time as an enemy, and from his face Lucian was worried about seeing Mithos with a black dragon. They were legendary. Mithos remembered what the old Master Rohnal said, that only after you have learnt the three divine spells and used them in combat will the black dragon come.

'Lucian, this is your last chance to surrender you know what it means when a black Dagon arrives.'

'I will never surrender to you, child, it is time you learnt your limitations. You may have learnt a couple of powerful spells but that is nothing compared to what I know.'

Lucian threw out his hands sending snaking purple light. Mithos focused magic in the path of the light, as the purple snake hit the dense air it bent to hit the roof of the palace, destroying a big chunk of the roof. Mithos sent a bolt of lightning towards Lucian which was warded.

Chapter Sixteen

Mathew sent a blade of air to sever the heads of soldiers who got too close to their line whilst his unit defended him. They fought in a ring. It was the best way to defend with Gilbert in the centre using a shield to stop any magic spell or arrow from getting to them. If Gilbert fell they would all die.

Mathew glanced up at the sky. In the setting sunlight he saw two dragons and between them coloured light flashed. He knew then what destroyed the roof. He saw several enemy soldiers looking up as well. The soldier to his left turned on Mathew, he just managed to move enough for the sword to miss a killing blow, but it caught his arm, the soldier behind killed Mathew's assailant but then turned to the enemy. Mathew sent more magic at the enemy then the flash of a red robe caught his eye. Mathew looked to see a man with black hair and brown eyes. This was one of Lucian's personal mages, he had to be one with special abilities, putting one and two together the soldier suddenly turning on him and his appearance. Mathew focused his power on the one in the red robe, the man brought up a shield.

'Saterans, stop the attack and get behind me,' the man said.

'Stand down,' Mathew said. The man in the red robe walked forward, Mathew walked to meet him in the middle of the battlefield.

'My name is Fear one of the three plagues of humanity.' Mathew finally knew the name of one of Lucian's favourite mage generals.

'I am warlock Mathew, I am the man who killed you.' Mathew drew his sword, no shield can stop a draining enchantment. So he charged at Fear swinging when the sword hit Mathew saw he had cut one of his own men in half, but the look of the blood said the man died a while ago. Mathew turned to see Fear behind him, then he looked back and saw he was facing his own soldiers. At some point he had gotten turned around and he was sure he had killed Fear.

Mathew turned back to face Fear again, this time he knew he was facing the right way, but he was surprised to see the ring of his men again and Gilbert in the centre looking tired, he was still holding the shield, Mathew turned again to see Fear. How were things changing round so often? Mathew sent a blade of air howling towards Fear who looked at the air wide-eyed as the blade cut him in half. Mathew was then shocked to see Gilbert cut in half.

Mathew felt something sharp in his back, it was a dagger, it missed any vital organs or arteries. Mathew, angered, finally realized Fear's power. It was illusion magic, a powerful form of it to trick a powerful mage. Mathew saw Fear behind him he knew if he attacked what he saw as Fear he would kill one of his own. He had already been fooled into killing one of his friends.

Mathew closed his eyes, they were no use in this, he had to use what he learnt from Lucian, he had to Sense the mana when Fear used his power. He followed the flow of power till it took a form, Fear was behind him, but all his other senses told him that the enemy was in front of him. Mathew finally knew how the power worked, the spell worked like a virus seeping into his eyes ears and nose changing everything, he saw heard and smelt but it didn't work on his power. Mathew focused the power down the full edge of his blade, he span sending a huge blast of edged air to the enemy.

Mathew opened his eyes and saw all the enemy troops on the floor cut in half, the mages didn't have time to put up a shield, they had all put their faith in Fear who was also separated from his legs.

'How did you do that?' Fear asked.

'You can fool my eyes my nose and even my ears but not my inner power, you were a fool to rely on that power alone,' with those words, Fear closed his eyes in death.

Mathew dropped to his knees at seeing Gilbert cut in half, he thought he might throw up, one of the soldiers approached him.

'Sir, we must press on, we understand you were being tricked by the magic. We must fight now and grieve later.' Mathew looked up to see more soldiers coming, Mathew looked to his men then back to the enemy.

'From here on we will fight more powerful enemies. Mathew charged into the enemy lines scything through them like death in a rage.

Mathew and his men finally killed enough of Lucian's soldiers for the rest to surrender. Mathew was tempted to kill them anyway, but then he remembered what Mithos said, 'If we don't accept their surrender then the war will never end,' Mathew looked up and saw the two dragons.

'I accept your surrender, but I wish you to change sides and serve Mithos Rohnal.'

171

The soldiers went to a knee and they swore their loyalty to Mithos. The soldiers looked in the same place he did.

'Mithos is on the black dragon, be thankful you aren't closer to that battle, the wasted magic alone would atomize you since you are unprotected.'

The flashes of magic seemed to split the sky it was a beautiful sight, but Mathew knew how deadly that beauty truly was.

Finally, Mathew took his eyes from the battle, they had to finish the job and force the enemy to surrender and there were still two special mages left, both would be stronger than Fear and Mathew didn't know what frightening powers they had.

Neji and Seon made their way through the centre of the palace, they didn't know how they were to find Mithos in such a huge palace Like Ariha, they had chosen not to take any soldiers with them, Neji thought they would get in the way. The further they walked they met more and more resistance but it was nothing they couldn't handle, the biggest challenge they faced was a group of ten black mages and that only lasted five minutes. Neji knew that they were both tired around a corner they saw a man with red hair and completely white eyes, it was a man in red robes with black flames on them. Neji and Seon stopped just short of the man. Neji kept Seon behind him, he couldn't let her of all people die. 'I am Neji, prince of the Shadow Reapers.'

'I am Pain, how well do you know me?'

Neji didn't understand the question, 'I do not know you at all,' Neji answered.

'You shall soon know pain,' Pain said. As he held out his hand Neji felt an odd pull and he was dragged from his feet. When he was close enough Pain unleashed a mighty blow punching Neji in the face. Pain raised his hand, smashing him into the ceiling and creating a huge hole in it.

Neji coughed, as he stood from the floor he discovered several ribs were broken. Neji glanced to Seon and saw that there was another man, they looked the same, they had the same smile.

'You will both know Pain, it is the force that binds all life, it is the one thing that all men and women can understand. A true universal language,' the two men said as one in the same deep voice.

Neji heard a snap as Seon collapsed to the ground, she was alive but both her arms were broken, with those injuries she couldn't help him and he would now have to fight two of them when it only took one of them to throw him around like a rag doll.

The two Pains approached slowly, they put their hands together with their index fingers making a triangle shape. Neji saw it, their mana took on two more forms. Four men all the exactly same, they all ran at him their robes billowing out behind them. When they got close enough they held out their right hands and unleashed a high pressure of air around him, it was like being crushed by four walls, he couldn't believe how fast they were. Neji felt his bones creaking and when the Pain faded the world went dark.

The four Pains turned to Seon, her arms were broken, she felt a cold chill behind herself, she turned to see a man in the same robes as Pain, he was handsome with a small scar crossing over his right eyebrow, his hair was a blue almost like lightning, but it was his blood-red eyes with the strange patterned hat that scared her. The man stopped short of her, unbuttoned his coat and crossed his arms. 'Pain, you may have gone too far with that one,' the man said as he pointed at Neji. 'You almost killed him.'

Seon turned her gaze to the four men; they were looking at Neji. Three of them vanished.

'I am sorry, Lord Death,' said Pain.

Seon turned to the man with blue hair, 'Hurry up and heal him enough so that he will wake up in a couple of minutes, we need him and his friends to occupy Lucian, I will heal the girl.'

Seon felt her bones crack back in place and as the bone knitted together she was finally able to move again. It was clear that these men were much stronger than Mithos and Lucian; she had to wonder why they served him. Pain went to join the one named Death, a smile came to his handsome face, 'Keep going in the direction you were going and you will come to a tall tower, Lucian and Mithos are fighting,' Death said, When Pain was done healing Neji he stood and walked to Death.

'What should we do about the woman?' Pain asked.

'Leave her, she will wait for the boy and carry on with him.'

With that, Death started off down the way that she and Neji had come. Seon sat with Neji for a while thinking about what had happened, those two men served Lucian, but Pain was so much stronger than her and Neji, he took them down with ease, but the way he took orders from Death meant he must be much stronger. What sort of demons had Lucian found? Seon thought.

Neji groaned and his eyes opened 'What happened?'

'That man Pain he defeated us with ease, then another man came and gave him orders, his name was Death and it seems like they might be using Lucian,' Seon replied.

Neji stood, he knew Pain had broken his ribs but the pain was gone, 'What happened why didn't they kill us?' Neji asked as he worked his joints.

'Death said they had things to do and they are counting on us keeping Lucian busy and they said that Mithos is already fighting Lucian,' Seon answered.

'I know that Mithos is fighting, I can feel his magic they have both summoned beasts to aid them.' Neji looked down the hall that Death told her to go down. 'They are that way we must hurry.'

Mithos Raised a shield round his dragon to block Lucian's barrage of fire and energy attacks; it was clear that Lucian was well-practiced with his dragon, their timing was perfect. When Lucian had to rest the dragon seemed to know it, the dragon would blast him with dragon's fire.

'What are you doing, Mithos, he is beating you back, your mana is running too low,' Master Rohnal said.

Mithos couldn't think of what he could do, he needed to use his mana to maintain the shield and with the strength of shield needed his dragon couldn't attack since it would bring down or destroy the shield, holding the shield Mithos knelt down closer to the dragon.

'David I need you to get us closer to them, if I can get on Lucian's dragon and force him in to a one on one fight I can beat him,' Mithos said.

'As you wish,' David the black dragon said.

David flew in close to Lucian's dragon, but it wasn't close enough.

'Closer, David!' Mithos yelled as the dragon turned for a second attack. Lucian had already started his next attack, throwing streams of lightning at him. David dodged each strike by tilting. When the strikes stopped David charged; by folding his wings back he dived towards the red dragon.

When David got close enough, he grabbed the red dragon with his mighty talons. Mithos ran up the length of

David's neck and jumped landing on the back of the red dragon. Mithos drew his knife and lunged for Lucian who grabbed Mithos's wrist, as the two dragons bit and clawed at each other Mithos and Lucian were locked in a battle of strength.

The dagger's path was headed straight for Lucian's heart, he span Mithos's hand round, Mithos used the speed of the spin to rotate in an attempt to hit his kidneys, but Lucian jumped back, Mithos focused mana into the blade and threw the knife at Lucian who erected a small shield at the point of the knife rebounding it, the knife spun and fell to the ground.

Mithos had to think fast, then the thought came to him. He was on Lucian's dragon Mithos focused mana to the soles of his feet allowing him to stick to the dragon and he placed his hands on the dragon's back and sent a web of black lightning into the dragon's back. The red dragon roared throwing its head back in pain. David went for its throat, ripping it out. Mithos jumped to David's back, Lucian ran to the red dragon's wing cutting off a piece of the thin membrane and using it to catch the air Lucian glided towards the roof of the tower. His dragon fell to the floor, without the use of both wings it hit the floor with a heavy thud.

Chapter Seventeen

Mithos stood on his dragon looking down at Lucian who threw the strip of flesh aside and stood ready to begin the battle again. Mithos had the advantage with his dragon, he crouched down and whispered to David, 'I am going to fight Lucian on the tower, I need you to circle the tower and attack him from every direction and I will attack from the ground,' Mithos said.

'David and conquer,' David said as he flew lower and Mithos jumped off.

Mithos faced Lucian, his aura glowed pure black and it crackled with power, the sign of a black aura meant that his will had been completely turned to darkness and it was powerful, within the black aura filled with a blood red cloud it swirled around him shifting. Mithos remembered reading something about this, but he couldn't remember what it meant.

Lucian drew his knife and cut his own hand bringing a strong flow of blood, it splattered on the ground, Lucian waved his hand with enough force to send more blood to the floor in a crescent shape. Lucian smiled it wasn't a grin of amusement but of bloodlust, blood dripped from Lucian's hand, he lifted it, the blood on the ground started to rise and solidify, each drop of blood came to a point.

'Do you know what magic this is?' Lucian asked.

'Blood magic,' Mithos replied.

'Yes, it is blood magic, but since it is using my own blood, blood invested with magic the same magic that it has always lived with, it makes the blood more powerful immune to attacking magic.'

Mithos erected a shield as the small projectile drops of blood shot at him. Each broke on the shield, they disintegrated on contact, but each drop of blood that hit weakened the shield. Mithos looked at Lucian's hand and saw he was using magic to keep the wound open, so more blood would trickle out at will.

Lucian's blood projectile assault stopped just before the shield collapsed, he was looking a little weak he had lost a lot of blood.

'You are better then I remembered, but tell me why haven't you used the divine spells in a while?'

'Because each use weakens me and my ability to fight, that is why I have only used two of the spells once.'

Lucian raised his hand to the sky. 'With this I will finish you, Blood of life and death I call to you come to me and give me strength I demand the power to conquer all, make me death incarnate.'

Blood rose from all around, rivers of blood from the dead in the palace. Mithos looked around as the blood walls gathered above them. It seemed like the battle was planned, Lucian needed enough dead to give him power. When people lived their blood was their own, but once dead it was there for any blood mage to claim.

When the blood finished rising and the walls were gone, Mithos looked up and saw the blood had taken the form of a roof above them. Suddenly a column of blood dived to Lucian coating him, it began to take on a mass and form of its own, the shapeless mass started to take form growing huge arms and legs, bone and grey flesh appeared where Lucian's flesh had been. As the blood vanished into the creature Lucian had become Mithos was almost sick from the sight and fetid smell of the beast, its arms legs and torso were heavily muscled, its right hand was nothing but an elongated bone sword, the left palm was covered in sharp razor teeth, it had no neck that Mithos could see, its two eyes had pupils like that of a toad and the mouth was round and filled with layers of needle like teeth.

Mithos held out his hand calling his sword to him.

'Let me fight him I could use some exercise,' the double voice of his evil half said, the last thing Mithos wanted was to let that loose cannon roam free in the world even if it was to kill Lucian.

The creature charged at him. It was a huge creature; each step shook the ground. Mithos dived under its sword, too late Mithos saw the tail covered in blades that seemed to be made of blood, using his mana, Mithos lifted himself just enough to dodge the blades as they swung.

The creature turned to back hand him, Mithos felt a rib break as the muscular arm made contact sending him flying.

'What the hell is that thing?' Mithos asked holding his broken rib.

'It is a bloodlust leach, they are demons that require a lot of blood to summon and it comes at the sacrifice of your soul,' Master Rohnal said in Mithos's head.

Mithos made a triangle hand sign to create two clones one of the clones launched a barrage of fire and lightning attacks the demon held its arm in a defensive stance and opened six slits in its arm, blood oozed out from the slits and solidified as a shield. The demon held up the shield to block the attack the first clone kept up the attack as Mithos and his second clone ran behind it, the second clone summoned daggers from a storage crest and started throwing them a third eye opened on the back of its head it used its tail to block the daggers.

Silently Mithos snuck up on the demon focusing mana through the blade to give it a sharper edge he swung the sword and severed the tail, as the tail fell to the floor the beast gave out a mighty cry it was an otherworldly scream almost like the scream of a hundred tormented souls, the second clone threw more daggers they hit the target stabbing the demon in the back.

The Demon howled all the more with each stab wound; dark blood leaked from the openings. With its attention distracted by the pain Mithos and his two clones unleashed blasts of fire lightning and energy, the three blasts blew up a thick layer of dust that ignited causing an explosion, the blast wave knocked Mithos over it had also zapped the last of his clone's strength causing it to vanish.

Neji and Seon met Mathew, Rin and Orden outside the tower, there were only a few soldiers with them and Gilbert was missing.

'Where is Gilbert?' Seon asked.

Mathew looked down, 'He didn't make, it I fought against Fear and killed him, but Gilbert was caught in the cross fire, the rest of the soldiers have escorted the enemy who surrendered,' Mathew said.

'Where is Areha?' Neji asked.

'She refused to wait and ran in to the tower,' Orden answered.

Neji shook his head, 'How powerful was Fear?' he asked Mathew.

'He had power over illusion magic, it affected all five scenes when I found that out he was easy to defeat.' Matthew explained.

'Well at least we know how weak he really was,' said a light, gentle voice. They turned to see two men in red trench coats with black flames sewn on. Mathew thought it was strange that one of them had red hair and the other had blue but there was no mistake who they were.

'What do you think, Pain?' Death asked.

'Well if he was that weak they did us a favour,' Pain said in his booming deep voice.

Neji drew his sword as did everyone else.

Death smiled, 'Reaper, the last time you tangled with Pain and his clones what happened?'

Neji flinched at the memory of being assaulted on four sides and seeing Seon with her arms broken. Neji sheathed his sword and motioned for the others to do the same

The two men walked forward looking up at the top of the tower like the soldiers, seeing the cloud of dust.

'Pain, it is almost time say what you came here to say then we have to put the plan into action,' said Death as he sat on a piece of rubble fallen from the fight upon the tower.

Pain turned to Neji and approached, 'You have great potential, I have the feeling that we will fight again, you must train hard to come up with a plan. Death and I have one hope and that is to find the warrior that can be our match in fighting ability and in magic power. I believe I have found mine as Death thinks he has found his possible match in Mithos, but he must see if he can beat Lucian.'

'Don't you two work for Lucian?' Mathew asked.

'No, we do not as he believes he was using us; we in fact were using him,' Death Said. Death stood. 'Pain, it is time, Lucian is getting desperate and we must ensure he dies in the right way.'

The two men started walking towards the entrance to the tower.

'WAIT,' Orden yelled.

Death and pain stopped just short of the entrance.

'Yes?' they said as one.

'Why do you want Lucian to die?'

Death turned, 'It is what our true master demands. For his plan to work Lucian must die and I am here to ensure he dies the right way. Pain is here to assist me in that by taking care of any interference so if you don't want to die don't get in my way.' With those last words, Death and Pain entered the tower.

Mithos watched as the dust settled. He put everything in that last attack, he had few spells more powerful than the three he unleashed with the help of his clones. Ariha came out from the opening in front of him. 'Ariha, get out of there,' Mithos yelled. Mithos focused on the dust cloud, there was movement in it, too late, Mithos saw the tentacle. 'What the hell is going on?' Mithos asked.

'The blood lust leach has two forms, the second form is much worse,' answered Master Rohnal.

The tentacle grabbed Ariha, Mithos could hear her bones cracking. When the rest of the dust settled, Mithos saw the huge form Lucian had now taken. 'My teacher, what have you done?' Mithos thought.

Lucian looked to be taller since his legs had split into eight tentacles; each had small spikes, thick bone armour ran up his back and the eyes were that of a snake – but the stench didn't change. Mithos conjured an axe and threw it at the tentacle that held Ariha severing it, Mithos used his mana to increase his speed and dashed to retrieve Ariha and carry her back to the other side of the entrance to the tower.

Ariha was lucky she had no broken bones, though she did have cuts on her arms where the black Shadow Reaper outfit was ripped by the sharp spikes on the tentacle. She opened her eyes he couldn't deny she was a true beauty. She turned to look at Lucian.

'Is that Lucian?' asked Ariha.

'Yes, he is using blood magic. I had hoped that I could talk him out of this and only give up his magic, but now I know he is beyond reasoning. He abandoned his reason when he used blood magic, he must now be destroyed,' Mithos answered.

Mithos looked up to see David flying above them. Mithos must have been too close for him to attack from the sky but now Mithos was at a distance and David was free to attack. He dived and blasted dragon fire at Lucian. From a normal red dragon the heat was intense but from a black dragon it was beyond intense, it was a blue flame and from the knowledge Mithos was given by Master Rohnal he knew how devastating it could be. Mithos leant close to Ariah, 'Do you have anything that could be used to attack from a distance?'

'No for Shadow Reapers battle is done face to face, the magic we use is only good at short distance, all I can do for long distance is to summon the mist, but there isn't enough moisture to bring on a thick fog that could help.'

When David's flame extinguished Mithos unleashed a blast of purple energy, as it hit Lucian it exploded 'Ariha, let's go!' Mithos yelled as he drew his sword. Ariha drew hers and they charged towards the beast. As they reached the area were they last saw Lucian, Ariha and Mithos swung till they hit the monster with, the mana in Mithos's sword it created a shock wave that blew away the cloud of dust.

Tentacles thrashed around, striking out, Mithos cut off the ones that came too close. He saw Ariha lying on the ground unconscious, he turned his vision back to Lucian, to the monster he had become and dived over a tentacle.

'David, take Ariha to safety!' Mithos yelled. The Dragon loosed another stream of fire at Lucian as he dived to Ariha. As David flew up to take her to safety the monster gathered energy to the palm of its hand, the energy grew in a flat round disk, Lucian threw the disk it was connected to a thin chain of energy. The disk severed one of David's wings then as it was pulled back the disk cut open David's side.

Mithos watched as David plummeted to the ground he could also see that he released Ariha. Mithos turned back to Lucian; in his anger he felt his restraint over his evil half slipping, if he lost any more concentration he knew that his dark side would take control and there would be no stopping him. Mithos had to calm down, this is the battle he had been training for, thousands had died to get him here at this place, Marik had given him power, he had to use it. Mithos closed his eyes, he sensed that Lucian was moving towards him.

Mithos opened his eyes sending the black fire lightning and wind at him it all hit Lucian at once sending a shriek like that from the underworld, the wind severed all of the tentacles and limbs whilst the fire and lightning burned through him. Mithos watched as the spells stopped, all that was left of the monster was a burnt carcass it started to split and crack, suddenly the burnt form exploded and Lucian appeared, his long hair tumbling over his shoulders and half his face burnt, his flesh melted.

'You fool,' Lucian hissed. 'What have you done to me, you damned child, I will be a god and you dare to fight me.'

It was clear that Lucian had gone mad. Mithos had lost all respect for his former master when he turned to Blood magic, not only did it eat away your mana but your soul as well.

'Lucian not only have you killed every mage in the academy but you have also killed the warlocks, but you didn't stop there you murdered the ruler of Satera then you brought war to innocent people and the worst of it you delved into blood magic,' Mithos said, unable to keep the rage from his voice.

Two men came from the opening in the roof of the tower one with blue hair and one with red hair but both wore the red trench coats with black flame that Lucian's inner circle was known for, they stood between Mithos and Lucian. 'This is great, I had Lucian, he was finally weak and now he gets back-up,' Mithos thought.

'What do you think you are doing?' Lucian asked they didn't answer, the two men turned to face Lucian.

'It is time for you to die, Lucian,' the one with blue hair said.

'What the hell are you talking about? You serve me!'

'No, we have a different master, we waited for the right time to put our plan into action,' the man with the red hair said with a deep voice.

'What master?' Lucian asked.

'Stand back, Pain this is my task,' the one with red hair bowed and moved to Mithos's side. The one with blue hair faced Lucian; they stared at each other.

'Watch closely, we thank you for bringing Lucian here, but he still has reserve mana and we can see that you are out. That man is Death, he has always had more power than Lucian, but he needed to get him here. Now watch as Lucian dies,' Pain said.

Lucian picked up Ariha's sword as he charged at Death who drew a sword of his own, but he kept his other hand in his pocket, Lucian swung with all his might but his blade was blocked with ease. Death side-stepped Lucian to let his momentum take him a step further. Death spun to slash Lucian's back; Lucian turned to face Death and focused mana to the palm of his hand and through the blade of his sword. Lucian threw the raw mana at Death who moved fast spinning to dodge the mana, then before Lucian could swing his sword, Death cut off Lucian's sword arm. Mithos had never heard such a scream. He knew it wasn't just from the cut but the charged mana burning him as well.

Chapter Eighteen

Death spun cutting off Lucian's other arm before placing the palm of his hand on Lucian's forehead. Death smiled.

'So that's what it was, the former Lord Rohnal was your older brother and that boy is your nephew,' Death said. Mithos couldn't believe what he had just heard because he didn't know who his parents were, but he respected Lucian, so much so that he took Lucian's last name as a symbol of respect. Death sheathed his sword and gripped Lucian by the scruff of his neck and dragged him to the glowing red altar. Mithos saw bones by the bottom of it.

Lucian tried to stop as Death dragged him. He was betrayed and it would cost him his life. They stopped just short of the altar. Why would Death kill him this way? Lucian thought.

Death leant in. 'You die in the name of your god, Marrik.' With that Death shoved Lucian in the altar, he saw the light surround him then the pain came, he felt his blood boiling and his skin and flesh melt. He was able to let out a last scream before his life faded.

Mithos saw Death walk away from the altar towards him and Pain. He stopped just short of them.

'Pain our work is done here, we must return for our next mission.'

Pain bowed and followed as Death left. Mithos descended the tower and was surprised to see Mathew, Orden, Seon, Neji and Rin with their soldiers and many of the enemy Sateran soldiers; all of the soldiers dropped to a knee. Neji was holding Ariha. To his relief Mithos saw that she was alive if a little beaten.

'The dragon saved me, he sacrificed himself for me,' Ariha said.

Mithos looked to David. His corpse anyway. Mithos performed the hand signals and chant to send him back home where the noble dragon could be buried by his own kin.

Mithos with his friends walked through the palace. The soldiers walked behind him. As they left the palace Mithos saw his own army with the Elves, but behind them was a larger force of Sateran soldiers.

'All Sateran forces are to be brought back home and I want messengers sent to the other academies – Manta Academy is to be rebuilt so we might teach those with magic. It is to be built here in Satera.'

The generals bowed. 'It would be our honour My Lord,' they said as one.

Mithos turned to his friends.

'I am the last of the Rohnal family, one with the Rohnal blood, you can all stay here and so can the army till they are rested. We need to talk about an alliance that will lead to a lasting peace.'

All his friends smiled with the war and the struggle finally over.